D0715559

WHISPERING SKULL

In search of work, cow-puncher Jeff Stewart is heading south. Making his way through the strange, untamed landscape that fringes the arid desert, he is riding up into the maze of canyons when there is distant gun-fire and a massive explosion. With the sound of bullets ringing in his ears, the naïve cowboy has no idea that the savage Barton gang is en route to the notorious prison, Fort Addams, to free their leader — and that soon Stewart and the gang will be on a deadly collision course . . .

DEAN EDWARDS

◆

WHISPERING SKULL

Complete and Unabridged

LINFORD
Leicester

First published in Great Britain in 2012 by
Robert Hale Limited
London

First Linford Edition
published 2014
by arrangement with
Robert Hale Limited
London

A catalogue record for this book is available
from the British Library.

ISBN 978–1–4448–2102–4

*Dedicated to the memory of
my friend Gene Autry.
The cowboy.*

Prologue

Utah was no place for angels and few were ever found within its harsh unforgiving boundaries. Hardened outlaws, however, were plentiful as they used its brutal terrain to outwit those who might try their luck in collecting their bounty. The vast untamed land was filled with sandstone mountains which appeared almost pink in the merciless rays of a sun that never seemed to quit. A thousand uncharted canyons stretched off in every direction between the high peaks. Yet the territory was also a land of contrasts that defied any logic known to rational minds. Apart from the mountains of strange rock formations which had the appearance of giant playing-cards that had toppled over there was also a lake. A lake of pure salt crystals which, it was said by those whose brains had been fried beneath the relentless sun, went on for ever.

This was not a land for cowards to venture into, for it took no prisoners. Those who thought they had it figured usually ended up nothing more than bleached bones.

This was a mysterious place, which it paid to steer clear of unless you had a very good reason not to. The six horsemen who waited at the edge of the salt lake amid the rocks beside the water hole, had such a reason. They were seasoned outlaws who were hell-bent on freeing their leader from the prison he had been sent to. A prison not ten miles from where they were watching the approaching mule train. It was not loyalty to Jardine Barton that had brought them to this perilous land. They had only one reason for their actions: a far more lucrative one than mere loyalty.

They wanted to discover the secret about the Whispering Skull. Their absent leader, Barton, had hooked them all long before they had reached this place, where they watched the mule train of covered wagons approach. His tall tales and the promise to take them to the Whispering Skull and share its untold treasure with them had ensured they would risk their very lives to rescue their leader. For Barton had told them that he was the only man alive who knew how to reach the Whispering Skull.

Greed had ensured their loyalty.

Each had their own theory as to what treasure waited for them somewhere amid the labyrinth of rocks. For years their leader had kept them on a hook like a master angler. Barton had plundered the very souls of his men by playing upon their avarice.

Sharky Cole was the man who had kept the others in check since their leader was captured. He alone knew how to ensure the others did exactly as he instructed. The faded three stripes on his weathered sleeves ensured his voice was louder and more chilling than

3

those of any of the others. The war might have ended years earlier but men like Cole never lost any of the volcanic threat that only cavalry sergeants ever achieve.

Cole looked at the others and nodded. He had told them all what they had to do. The men feared Cole far more than their enemies' bullets. They would obey without a second thought and do what he had told them to do.

His wrath was something they had all tasted. It was of a flavour that no one wanted to taste again for it savoured of blood.

'Mount,' Cole said. He turned and grabbed the reins and mane of his horse. He stepped into the nearer stirrup, swung up on to his saddle and then steadied his mount as the others copied his actions. 'Them wagons will be here within ten minutes. They only got three outriders guarding the three wagons, boys. Ya knows what I told ya.'

Pecos Bill eased his horse around the

large water-hole towards the narrow-eyed Cole. He gave a nod. 'Me and Rance will take out the riders.'

Rance Lee gave a chuckle. 'We'll kill 'em before they even has time to know that they're in trouble, Sharky.'

Cole drew a deep breath and glanced at the others. He pointed at them.

'Elroy will ride wide and kill the driver of the last wagon as Bo and Tey take the first and second ones. I want them drivers killed fast and sweet, boys. Fast and sweet.'

Elroy Elam, Bo Harper and Tey Tyler all nodded as they leaned forward over the necks of their horses and stared at the wagon train of vehicles cutting through the haze across the white salt. They all knew that the water hole behind them was where the sunbaked wagons were headed.

'What you gonna be doing when we is all killing them varmints, Sharky?' Rance Lee asked as he checked his guns.

'I'm gonna be killing all the folks you

boys only wing,' Cole replied coldly. 'I'm gonna finish off any one of them bastards ya fail to finish off permanent. Savvy?'

'Sure enough.' Lee nodded.

The supply wagons were being drawn by six mules apiece. Each wagon was laden down with a month's supplies of everything the distant fortress required. Food, drink and ammunition were the bulk of their cargo.

Cole looked at Pecos Bill and Lee and waved his free hand at them. 'Now.'

The two outlaws drove their spurs deep into the flesh of their horses and thundered away from the rocks. As ordered, the riders fanned out to either side of the approaching wagons.

Cole then looked at the three others.

'Remember, boys. Fast and sweet.'

Elam rode through the dust left in the wake of their two companions. He hung low across the neck of his galloping mount as both Harper and Tyler followed.

A smile etched the face of Sharky

Cole; a sickening smile such as only hardened killers could ever muster. He spun his reins and whipped the tail of his horse. The animal leapt into action and raced after the five others.

Before Cole had reached even the noses of the mules of the first wagon he could hear the shooting starting. As Tyler blasted three bullets into the belly of the wagon driver Cole sent a perfectly placed bullet into the man's head. Even before the dead driver had fallen from his high perch Cole had reached the second wagon and finished off the wounded driver who was scrambling away from Harper's bullets.

Another perfectly placed bullet sent the man flying off the driver's board. His body crashed on to the traces and under the hoofs of the nervous mules.

Abruptly Cole drew rein and waited for the third of the wagons to reach him. His cruel eyes saw that there was no call for him to waste any more bullets. Elam had made short work of its driver. Cole watched as the outlaw reached up, grabbed the collar of the dead driver and hauled him off the seat. The body crumpled into the pristine white salt. Elam then placed a boot on his saddle and mounted the wagon. He retrieved its reins and eased the mules to a stop.

'That was too damn easy, Sharky.' Elam laughed out loud. 'I seen me churchgoing females that put up a better fight than these critters.'

Cole spurred and rode to where the bodies of the dead guards lay. Their blood spread across the white ground. An even wider smile filled Cole's features as he thrust his gun back into its holster.

'Fast and sweet.' Cole swung his horse around. 'Git these mules watered. Wash every drop of blood off these wagons. We don't want nobody to figure out what we done, do we?'

His men obeyed.

Sharky Cole spat and then looked at the bulging cargo beneath the canvas of each of the vehicles. He rose in his stirrups and pointed at Pecos Bill.

'Bill, I want every damn thing on the first wagon dumped,' he shouted loudly. 'Then ya fills it with them gunpowder barrels we got hid up in the rocks.'

Pecos Bill waved a hand in reply.

'Gonna make one hell of a big bang, Sharky,' Rance Lee said as he reloaded his .45.

'That's for sure,' Cole agreed.

'When we get Barton out of that place do ya reckon he'll take us to the Whispering Skull?' the younger outlaw queried.

Cole looked at Lee. 'He sure better, coz if'n he don't I'll kill him with my bare hands, Rance. Fast and sweet.'

1

Fort Addams prison had once been, as its name implied, nothing more than a cavalry outpost set in the arid Utah wastelands. It had been built to keep the natives at bay, yet the half-starved Shoshoni Indians had gone even before the fort had been completed leaving the sprawling sandstone and adobe structure redundant before its potential could actually be utilized. It did not take long before the powers that be back East realized that with a few minor alterations they had constructed a perfect place to jail the growing population of outlaws which was overflowing from their other prisons.

A perfect prison had been constructed totally by accident.

Set close to the jagged mountain ranges of pure weathered stone mesas and situated on the edge of a vast salt lake that seemed to go on for ever, Fort Addams had proved its worth many times over the handful of years since its cells were filled with the most notorious of men who had somehow avoided the hangman's noose but soon came to wish they had not. Many condemned outlaws were sent to Fort Addams just to be hanged, for it was far away from the increasingly critical eyes of newspaper reporters.

Because of its remoteness and twenty-feet-thick walls the prison had quickly been considered impenetrable and escape-proof. Many convicts had attempted to escape from the sun-bleached edifice and had been shot down by its guards. Those who had somehow managed to escape from inside the prison soon found that the terrain beyond was just as deadly as the bullets of the men who patrolled the prison's high walls.

Bare rations and hard labour soon accounted for those prisoners who were neither blessed with youth, health or good fortune. This was an unholy place. A place built by Satan when the Almighty had had his back turned. So far none of its inmates had survived their sentences but the outside world did not know or care. For these evil creatures deserved everything they got.

A more brutal place in which to imprison men could not have been found anywhere. In the years since it had accepted its first prisoners not one of them had managed to buck the odds and escape alive. Every outlaw knew that to be sent to serve time at Fort Addams was to have a death sentence bestowed upon your head. A rope noose would be far more favourable.

Yet even the most robust of prisons is only as strong as its weakest link. The easiest way out of such a place is usually the very same as the way in.

No matter how thick the walls of any structure, it has to have a gate and gates are only as strong as the armed men who guard them. For men make mistakes. And it only takes one error of judgement in order to make twenty-feet-thick walls useless.

Of all the prisoners within the baking-hot cages inside Fort Addams there was one man who was unlike all his fellow inmates and his name was Jardine Barton.

Barton knew his time inside the prison was limited. The judge had told him so. He was there waiting to be hanged. The judge had decided that as Barton led one of the most infamous gangs in all of the territories it would be insanity to try and hold him in any normal town jail to await the building of his gallows. For Barton's ruthless gang of mercenaries were still on the loose, and they would never shy away from any average jail. These were conscienceless killers. Men who feared no star packers and would try and free Barton at any cost. They would also kill anyone who got in their way.

So the judge wisely decided the safest course of action was to send Jardine Barton to Fort Addams to be held for the thirty-eight days before his date of execution. Even a gang as hardened as Barton's would never try to free their leader from that unholy prison. Fort Addams was the one place that even Barton's gang would never be able to best.

Set away from the other buildings beneath the blazing rays of an unforgiving sun a small stone and adobe cage had been constructed. It was only five feet square inside its putrid interior and designed to make it impossible for its occupant either to stand or lie down. A locked door and a small barred window were the only features upon the stone and adobe.

Jardine Barton had been locked up inside its crippling confines for more than a week, knowing that each beat of his merciless heart drew him closer to the rope which would ultimately stretch and snap his neck.

His burning eyes stared through the small hole. It allowed him to see the white-hot sand between his private prison and the well-constructed gallows set right in the middle of the courtyard. The blocks of cells beyond appeared like paradise to the outlaw. He could just make out the start of the larger quarters built for his captors.

Soaked in his own filth Barton had grown more and more angry at the rarely seen warden and the brutal gun-toting guards, who were treating him as though he were nothing more than a rabid creature: a creature it was their duty to not only kill but humiliate. Each passing hour made the already heartless man even more deadly. In his mind he was killing each and every one of them a thousand times over.

They would all pay for this, he vowed.

Pay big.

Even brought down to the humiliation he was now wallowing in, Jardine Barton had never once doubted that his gang would not leave him here to be hanged.

They were coming. Coming soon to

free him and destroy his new enemies. Barton was certain of that. If nothing else, he was sure of that one single thing. His gang would be here soon to free him. Nothing could stop them.

It was not loyalty which would bring them here to this remote place but something far more compelling. Barton managed to chuckle to himself as he continued to peer through the small barred hole in the side of the stone cage.

His men had been promised something which would make them all richer than their wildest dreams. Something they would only be able to get their hands on if Barton was alive. For the outlaw leader Barton was the only man alive who knew the secret to where a fortune lay waiting for them.

He glared at the guards near the front gate on the high ramparts that surrounded the fortress. His men would soon be here, he told himself over and over. Soon they would break him free of the shackles which tormented both his body and his mind. Soon he would be able to turn the tables upon those who relished tormenting him.

His men were close. Barton could sense it. He knew that they could never allow him to die, because without him there was no chance of any of them finding the treasure he had promised to share with them. A treasure of which only he knew the whereabouts.

Jardine Barton knew the secret that would save his life.

The secret of the Whispering Skull.

2

A few miles from the salt flats young wrangler Jeff Stewart rose in his stirrups, turned his head and looked along the canyon in the direction in which his bandanna tails were fluttering in the gentle breeze. Bleached brush, more dead than alive, hindered even his keen eyes from seeing anything but swirling hot air. This was a place that mocked even the toughest and most youthful of souls. The cowboy chewed on his lower lip and then returned his shiny pants to the saddle. He considered the echoes of gunfire which were still bouncing off the high walls of jagged rock on either side of him. Somewhere close, men had been doing battle and the cowpoke felt uneasy. Anxiously he looked at the head of his trusty quarter horse. Its ears were still pricked and, like its master's, were vainly searching for the location of the gunmen.

They had both heard the brief gun battle but had no way of knowing from where the shots had originated. Sound travelled swiftly through the maze of canyons in these parts, Stewart told himself. The men who had been doing the shooting could be a hundred miles away or perhaps just beyond the swirling heat haze. A shiver traced his straight spine as his gloved hands took up the slack in his reins.

Stewart was nervous. He was no gunfighter, no gun for hire, as so many were in this desolate territory. He was a cowpuncher on his way south to find himself honest work before the winter set in. The cowboy kept chewing nervously on his dry, cracked lips and slowly turned the horse until its head was pointed in the direction they had been travelling before the ear-splitting gunshots had reached them.

'Easy, boy,' Stewart whispered to the mount as he toyed with his reins and held them to his belly. 'Reckon them shots come from a long ways back. Ain't no call for us to be feared.'

The young wrangler did not believe one word of his utterances but knew if he repeated them enough he himself might just come to believe them. So far he had been wrong.

When there was shooting in these parts some poor critter was getting itself brutally killed. Stewart knew that probably a whole bunch of poor critters were dead or dying behind him. Why they had fallen prey to deadly lead was troubling the youngster, for he knew that to some outlaws a man just having a half-decent horse under him was cause enough to make him a target.

His gloved hand drew the ancient Colt from its weathered holster. He opened its chamber and counted the six bullets which had been there since he had first purchased the .45 two years earlier. He then checked the belt strapped around his lean waist. Another ten bullets were dotted along it. There were gaps left by the previous owner who, like Stewart, had never bothered to buy any fresh ammunition to replace the spent ones.

There was a crack in the wooden grip of the weapon where Stewart had used the gun as a hammer rather than for what it had been intended. He swallowed hard.

'It better not come to a showdown coz I sure ain't no gunslinger,' Stewart mumbled, and dropped the gun back into its holster. He rubbed a sleeve across his dust-caked face. 'Reckon we better make tracks before one of them gun-toting varmints loaded for bear comes this way. I knows ya tuckered but we gotta put a lot of sand between us and them. C'mon, boy.'

Stewart eased the horse forward and allowed it to walk at its casual pace through the dry, white sandy draw. The sweat began to trail down the tanned face of the cowboy as he became more and more aware that the shots he had heard might have spewed from guns a lot closer than he had first figured. The gunman or men might be riding hard in the same direction as he was going.

Whoever it was doing the shooting might just still have themselves an appetite for more killing. A hankering for even more notches on their gun grips.

Stewart looked at the suds on his horse's shoulders. The horse was tired, but since hearing the shots it was also as skittish as its master.

The cowboy tapped his spurs.

The quarter horse responded and thundered forward.

★　★　★

Just as Barton had predicted, they were coming. In fact, they had already arrived at their destination. The whitewashed walls of Fort Addams reflected the vicious blinding rays of the sun until it looked like a gigantic jewel perched in the middle of the desolate terrain.

Each of the outlaws pulled his hat brim down to shield his dust-filled eyes from the dazzling display as, perched on the high drivers' seats, they aimed the mule train along the well-worn tracks towards the prison's massive gates.

The outlaws' own horses were securely tethered behind the tailgate of each supply wagon. They were unseen by the unsuspecting guards who patrolled the high walls and watched the approaching caravan. The guards had seen the familiar sight many times and were drooling in anticipation at having themselves some treats like fresh tobacco and kegs of beer. A month was an awful long time when you were stranded in the middle of a desert, reliant on everything apart from water being brought in by supply wagon.

Satisfied grins from the guards beamed upon the wagons.

But this delivery of provisions was not going to be like any of those which had preceded it. This one was going to be remembered by the prison officers for a long time. If they survived its delivery, that was.

Sharky Cole was guiding the first of the wagons as Elam rode alongside with his carbine resting on his right thigh. Both men were keeping their heads lowered just in case one of the onlookers recognized their hardened features. The second wagon was being driven by Pecos Bill whilst Lee rode escort. The last of the Conestoga wagons was being guided towards the prison by Bo Harper as Tyler kept level with him astride his almost white gelding.

Each man had a hand on a gun. Each hand had a finger on each weapon's trigger. Dust rose from the hoofs of the long line of mules as the sure-footed animals expertly negotiated the rugged trail towards the forbidding prison walls.

A lot of mules made an awful lot of dust. Clouds of it billowed up and washed over the watching guards. It was a bonus that Sharky had not considered when he had first come up with his deadly plan to free Jardine Barton before the outlaw was hanged.

Sharky pulled back on the hefty reins and watched as the team of six mules came to a rest. The noses of the lead mules were almost touching the secured gates as the outlaw on the driver's seat gave a wave of his hand to the heavily armed men upon the parapet. He then pulled out a long twisted cigar from his coat pocket and rammed it between his blackened teeth. He scratched a match along his pants leg, cupped its flame to the end of his smoke and sucked as his eyes surveyed the onlookers.

He inhaled and then blew the flame out before casually glancing at Elam. Both men smiled. It was the smile of death.

'Open up them gates if'n ya wants these provisions,' Sharky yelled out through the dust which was still rising from the hoofs of his team of mules.

'We got us a whole heap of salt pork back here just begging to be thrown on a griddle.'

One of the more alert of the guards leaned over the parapet wall and screwed up his eyes. He stared down at the deadly outlaw.

'Who is that?' the guard called down curiously. 'Is that you, Gabby? Sure don't sound like you.'

Sharky shook his head. 'Gabby took himself sick. I was mustered in to replace the old bastard at the last minute. Now git them gates opened up if'n ya wants to have this grub.'

The explanation and the demand seemed to work. The guard straightened up and started giving orders to the rest of the rifle-toting prison officers.

'Open up,' the guard ordered masterfully.

Again Sharky looked to Elam. Again they both smiled.

The sound of the heavy gates being opened filled each of the outlaws' ears. Slowly but surely the high gates parted to reveal the interior of the courtyard.

Sharky Cole raised a hand and gave a salute to the men on the high wall. They returned the empty gesture.

With one powerful hand Sharky lifted the reins and brought them down across the backs of the mules. The mules began to walk once more, hauling their heavy cargo behind them. The eyes of the outlaw darted all around as the animals slowly entered through the arched gateway.

He was surveying his prey.

Sharky knew that this fortress was meant to hold a couple of dozen guards and a few officers. His keen mind counted nearly that many within sight of his high driver's seat. He allowed the mules to find their own route towards the long bakehouse where black smoke trailed up from the blackened chimney. Sharky could smell the aroma of the evening meal being prepared as it wafted across the courtyard from the building's open windows.

The mules had been to the remote

prison many times. They knew where they had to go even if their driver did not, but Sharky had other ideas as to their destination. He looked back at the two trailing vehicles as their mule teams brought them into the heart of the prison courtyard. Sharky drew alongside the large whitewashed building that he recognized as being the officers' living quarters and arsenal. He pushed a hefty boot down on the brake pole. All six of the mules reluctantly came to a halt. Knowing that half of the wagon behind him was filled with barrels of black powder Sharky looped the reins around the pole and then gave a nod at Elam.

The rider dragged his reins hard and rode back to Sharky's horse which was tied to the long wagon's tailgate. Elam pulled its reins free and led the mount back to the second wagon, which had stopped in the very centre of the huge yard. The outlaw leaned from his saddle and secured the mount's reins next to Pecos Bill's horse. Elam then watched each of the three men drop down from their high perches. He was about to spur back to Sharky when he noticed the small cell of stone and adobe a few feet from the mules. It was stinking like an outhouse short on lime.

Elam drew his horse to a halt beside it. To his shock and surprise he saw the emaciated Barton gripping the bars of his tiny cell. He had never seen anything, apart from a hog in a sty, looking so pitiful before. Yet Barton's eyes still burned with fury.

'Git here, Elroy,' Barton snarled through his own filth.

'Jardine?' Elam gasped as he jumped down to the ground.

'I knew you boys would come for me, Elroy,' Barton said. 'Git me out of this stink hole. Shoot the lock off the door. Git me out of here.'

Elam straightened up and tried to look as though he were not talking to the caged outlaw. His eyes watched the guards who were closing the gates behind them.

'I can't free ya yet, Jardine,' Elam said.

'Why the hell not?' Barton growled.

'Believe me. Ya safer in there for the time being, boss.'

'What ya mean?' Barton turned his head. He could see Sharky puffing on his fresh-lit cigar. 'What's Sharky doing? Why ain't he started killing these bastards yet?'

'Sharky got himself a better idea,' Elam told him.

Barton shook at the bars. 'I'm the leader of this bunch. I make the plans.'

'Ya didn't make this'un,' Elam said.

'What's he got planned?'

'If I was you I'd hush up and duck down low and stay there, Jardine.' Elam led his mount to where the other men had gathered between the second and third wagons.

The five outlaws rested their aching backs against the tailgate next to the tied-up horses and waited. Only Elam watched from the corner of the second wagon as Sharky Cole blew at the tip of

30

his cigar until it glowed red. Then Sharky moved down the length of the wagon and pulled at a long fuse wire which was jutting out from its boarded side. The outlaw pushed the cigar against the end of the fuse. A puff of smoke was the only clue that the fuse had been ignited.

Elam discreetly drew his guns and watched as Sharky ran towards the rest of the gang.

'Where ya going?' one of the guards called out as more and more of them were drawn to the first of the supply wagons.

Sharky did not pause or reply.

He quickened his pace.

More guards ventured down from the high walls and gathered around the Conestoga wagon as was their monthly habit.

'Here he comes,' Elam informed the other outlaws as they pulled their weapons free of their holsters and cocked their hammers.

'He lit the fuse, Elroy?' Lee queried.

'Yep,' Elam answered coldly.

'Take cover,' Sharky yelled out to the rest of the outlaws. He threw himself across the last couple of yards and landed next to the wagon's rear wheel. He rolled frantically under the large vehicle, screwed up his eyes in fearful anticipation and pushed his gloved hands over his ears.

Then it happened.

Like an angry volcano too long dormant.

It was as though the world itself had exploded.

3

The world within the confines of Fort Addams was indeed exploding. Red shafts of devilish wrath spurted out in every direction as the burning fuse reached the first of the gunpowder barrels hidden in the wagon. In the space of a heartbeat another barrel joined the first and blasted out. All living things within a forty-foot radius were reduced to ash and the solid walls of the prison's buildings closest to the volcanic eruption were left smouldering ruins. The twenty-foot-long wagon had suddenly vanished amid the earth-shaking explosion, which had rocked the very foundations of the remote desert prison. One after another the barrels of gunpowder exploded, sending burning splinters of wood and cargo debris away from the huge crater. Flesh was torn from both men and animals closest to the violent roar. The stores of ammunition in the prison arsenal exploded, adding to the devastation. Bullets ripped up into the air as though a hundred unseen phantoms were firing their defiance at the gods. Billowing black smoke stuttered and curled out in all directions as if it were a strange monster once buried in the depths of a madman's imagination.

Fiery plumes of red venom flashed and spewed out like rods of satanic wrath. The guards who had been walking towards the wagon were gone, their bodies vaporized by the heat and sheer force of the unholy explosion. Parts of bodies had been thrown a hundred feet and burned as the meat was roasted off their shattered bones.

The entire prison shook as violent shock waves rolled from the source of the volcanic outburst. Its walls and buildings close to the explosion had been reduced to rubble; the remainder of the remote fortress lay cracked and blackened.

Choking black dust filled the area of devastation covering everything that remained standing. The pitiful sound of those mules that had somehow survived rang out like haunting songs from another world. Yet even as the dust continued to fill the courtyard and the ground continued to shake, Sharky Cole had crawled out from beneath the second wagon with both his guns drawn in readiness.

The dust kept on coming. It seemed to be alive, or like a wave of death that rolled over everything in its path driven by the last of the exploding barrels' powerful blasts. Even Sharky could not withstand the power of the force behind the cloud of dust that hit him.

The outlaw fell on to his back and tried to see, but there was nothing to see except the brown mass which covered him. He fought his way back to his feet and tried to fill his lungs with air, but it was impossible.

Then he caught the scent of death itself in the dust which filled his nostrils as well as his eyes. The abominable scent of dead men and beasts which had been ripped apart by the blast was everywhere. Grown men and muscular mules had been reduced to nothing more than sickening dust.

Dust that covered the outlaws. Dust that had managed to crawl into every pore of their bodies like an invasion of termites.

Sharky fell against the wagon as a brief gap in the choking dust allowed him to see the destruction he had just wreaked. He rubbed the dust from his face with the back of his gloved hands as they still held on to the grips of his guns. Half the mules of the second wagon had fared no better than those on the one he had driven up to the arsenal. What was left of them was little more than a mangled heap of scarlet gore pushed up over the still-living mules that had been closer to the body of the wagon itself.

Sharky spat and walked to where the other outlaws were huddled. His boots began to kick them into realizing that they were still alive.

'Git up,' Sharky coughed. 'We got us a few more guards to kill before this damn place is safe.'

Elam and the others got off their knees and shook the dust off their bodies as they tried to regain their senses.

'Sharky.' Barton's voice called out from the cesspit he was still caged in. 'Git me out of here. That's an order.'

Sharky ignored Barton's shouting and staggered forward with his weapons at hip level. He was angry now. Angry that Barton still considered himself their leader even though it had been Sharky who had masterminded this unholy outrage.

Suddenly the stumbling outlaw saw movement on the wall close to the gates. Two guards who had been knocked off their feet were rising with their carbines clutched firmly in their hands. The outlaw shuffled away from the wagon through the smoke and swirling dust towards the foot of the ladder next to the gate.

The guards were stunned. Neither man knew what had just happened and they were staggering to the top of the ladder. As the first grabbed hold of the ladder and stepped on to its top rung, Sharky fired both guns.

His bullets were deadly.

The lifeless guard fell limply to the ground.

The second of the guards swiftly raised his rifle, cranked its mechanism, aimed and squeezed its trigger. The rifle bullet went way over Sharky's head. The outlaw laughed and fired another fatal pair of shots upward.

The bullets tore into the belly of the guard. His hands dropped the rifle, then clutched at his guts. Blood trailed through his fingers as another volley of lead hit him in the face. No rag doll could have fallen with such ease as did the body of the guard. He toppled off the high wall and crashed into the sand at Sharky's feet.

Sharky spat. 'It don't pay to tangle with Sharky Cole.'

Then behind him all hell broke loose.

Suddenly shots were being fired in all directions. Sharky swung on his boot heels and cocked both his hammers once more. He could see Elam and the rest of his men using the second wagon as a shield whilst they returned fire to a few remaining guards who were running from the only building within the prison walls to have survived.

Bullets rained in on the wagon as the startled guards closed the distance between themselves and the outlaws. Chunks of wood flew heavenward as the bullets tore into the body of the wagon.

Totally unafraid Sharky walked slowly through the swirling soup of smoke and dust towards the approaching guards with his guns blazing in unison.

Before the guards had made it halfway across the debris-littered courtyard Sharky had managed to shoot and kill every one of them.

As he got to the side of the wagon Sharky snarled at the other outlaws.

'That's the way ya meant to do it, boys,' he drawled. 'Fast and sweet.'

The hardy Pecos Bill slid the sixth fresh bullet into his smoking gun chambers, snapped the weapon shut and spun the .45 on his trigger finger. He gave a grizzled look at Sharky, then led the others out into the choking air in search of more of the guards to kill. Within seconds their weapons were spitting lead at the handful of survivors. Only Elam remained beside Sharky. He watched as the older man shook the spent casings from his guns and replaced them with bullets from his belt.

'Ya figure there's many of these critters still left living, Sharky?' Elam asked.

Sharky holstered one of his reloaded guns as his thumb pulled back on the hammer of the other smoking .45.

'Let's take us a looksee, Elroy,'

Sharky answered. 'I figure the only bastards still sucking air around here besides us is them prisoners yonder.'

'We gonna free 'em?' Elam innocently enquired.

'Nope. Let 'em rot.' Sharky chuckled. 'I figure they'll sure die cussing us. Seeing these couple of wagons here and them not being able to get their hands on the provisions.'

'Ain't that kinda mean?'

'Yep.' Sharky nodded.

Both outlaws began to walk back towards the still-burning remnants of the wagon now reduced to splinters. In a few strides the four other outlaws had joined them. They were like vultures seeking out fresh carcasses.

With each stride the voice of Jardine Barton screaming behind them filled the toxic air.

'Git me out of here, ya bastards,' Barton yelled at the top of his lungs. 'Do ya hear me? Set me free.'

'Just keep ya eyes open for more prison guards, boys,' Sharky ordered as his boots started to sink into the deathly grime which covered the once white ground. 'If ya spots anyone still able to move a finger kill him.'

'Let me out of here,' Barton yelled again from his tiny cell set next to the bloody entrails of what had once been a dozen or more mules.

'He's getting kinda loud, Sharky,' Harper noted.

'Good.' Sharky spat as he kicked a boot aside. A boot which still had part of a leg inside it.

Elam stopped and looked back. 'He'll sure be mad when we lets him out. Mad as hell.'

'He always was.' Sharky spat again and continued to walk forward until he was satisfied that everything close to where the arsenal had once stood was dead. He paused and glanced over his shoulder at the rest of the outlaws.

'Old Jardine gotta learn that from now on I'm the head honcho of this bunch. I'm tired of waiting for him to keep his promise and take us to that treasure he bin harping on about for the last few years, boys. If he don't lead us to Whispering Skull from here, he's gonna be as dead as these pitiful *hombres* are.'

The outlaws all turned and walked slowly back towards the man wallowing in his own filth. A man who had no idea that his life was balanced on a knife edge.

4

The vast cloudless sky was beginning to turn red as the last of the day succumbed to the inevitable coming of night. It was as red as fresh-drawn blood and each of the riders knew that in an hour only stars would light their villainous path through the canyons of jagged peaks. Six of the seven horsemen were ready and eager to set off on their quest to find the place where they had been told their fortune awaited. Nothing but death itself could stop them this time. The seventh had no inkling that his days as their leader had ended, and that if he did not honour his word this time his hours of life were numbered. Dust rose from the hoofs of their sturdy mounts as the horsemen steered a route back down to where they had bush-whacked the caravan of supply wagons only a few hours earlier. Each of the riders knew he was getting close to their goal as the sickening scent of death grew more intense.

The haunting sound of the wailing prisoners still caged and held captive in their cells inside what remained of Fort Addams faded at last in the smouldering heat haze that surrounded them as Sharky Cole led them down through the mountainous pass to where they had left their supply wagon a few hours earlier. Beyond the rocks lay the desert of salt which beckoned all those who were loco enough to try and cross its uncharted immensity. Its crystallized surface sparkled as though a million precious jewels were spread for as far as the eye could see.

Blinding rays of the low-hanging sun dazzled the riders' eyes and reflected off the lake of white salt ahead of them. How many men and beasts had been lured out there to their deaths each of the outlaws secretly wondered? Only the blood and bodies of the six dead supply men lying upon the flat bed of salt tainted an otherwise perfect scene, but it was not the dried salt lake which would tempt these riders to risk their lives.

It was the range of lifeless sand-coloured mountains which held their fate. Somewhere within that hostile terrain Jardine Barton had told them he had once discovered a fortune. He had said that Whispering Skull was the key to finding it once more.

Yet what exactly was Whispering Skull?

Each of the outlaws had his own theory but Barton had never fully explained any details. Recently Sharky had wondered if there was such a place as Whispering Skull at all. Maybe the man who had led them for so many years had just invented the entire tall story to keep his men sweet. Now the hardened outlaw was determined to find out one way or another.

Sharky Cole would discover the truth.

As the horses were reined in, half a

dozen vultures lifted off the bodies they had been feasting upon and flew up to where the warm thermals allowed them to circle against the scarlet heavens.

Jardine Barton had not stopped talking since he had cleaned up and followed his men to where they had left their supply wagon. The outlaws had heard it all before and now they were determined not to fall for his skilful patter. They wanted only one thing: to be taken to the place where he had always told them their fortune awaited. Dust crept up from the hoofs of the riders' mounts as they came to rest beside their wagon. The wagon in which they had brought a deadly cargo of barrels of gunpowder.

Barton had continued to talk whilst his saviours remained totally silent and unimpressed around him. Naively Barton still believed he could keep leading them along as he had always done. But the hardened riders were no longer willing to be fooled with empty promises.

Promises they now knew would be broken.

Barton had always acted like a preacher in the pulpit, filling his congregation with promises of a better life if they just obeyed the rules. His rules. Just one more job and then just one more. Over and over again. Everything they had ever desired was there on the horizon and all they had to do was keep riding towards that distant goal.

Yet no matter how far a man rides he can never reach the horizon. It never gets any closer.

Sharky Cole and his fellow gang members had realized since their leader had been imprisoned that they could get on perfectly well without him. In fact Sharky had been far better at planning than Barton had ever been.

The outlaws said nothing as Barton continued to spew out his ambitious plans. Each of them watched one empty promise after another come from Barton's lips. Each outlaw festered with anger knowing that if he failed to lead them to the Whispering Skull this time, they would simply kill him.

The bull's ring was no longer in their noses and he was no longer able to control them. The strings of the puppets had been cut yet the puppet master was oblivious of the fact.

Now they watched with hatred burning like erupting volcanoes in their narrowed eyes. Each had already hatched his own personal plan as to how he would kill the jabbering Barton.

The riders dismounted from their mounts beside their wagon and watched both Sharky and Barton with interest. When would Sharky make his move? When would Barton realize that his days as their undisputed leader were over?

Sharky secured his reins to the wagon tailgate and pulled out a cigar from his coat pocket. He bit off its tip and spat it away. He gripped the long black weed between his teeth and sparked a match, cupped its flame and inhaled the smoke deep into his lungs. As smoke drifted through his stained and broken teeth Sharky stared at Barton with the same look he had given every man he had killed over the years.

Suddenly without warning Sharky spoke.

'Ya feel lucky, Jardine?' he asked through a cloud of smoke. He tossed the match over his shoulder. 'Do ya?'

Bewildered, Barton stopped and looked at Sharky. He then noticed that the others were all looking at *him*, each wondering what their new leader was about to do to their old one.

'Ya talking to me, Sharky?' Barton looked hard at the man he had spent years ordering about. For the first time since he had been rescued from Fort Addams Barton noticed that all of his men had a strange air about them. One he had never encountered before. It was gritty courage.

'Yep.' A slow nod came from the man with the cigar gripped in his dark teeth. 'Ain't nobody else around here called

Jardine, is there?'

Barton was still feeling frail after being confined in the small stone cell back at Fort Addams, but was determined to try and bluff the outlaw as to his capability. He tightened his stare.

'Sure I feel lucky. You boys saved me. Reckon I feel real lucky. Why'd ya ask, Sharky? Are ya figuring on us having a fight? I ain't as fit as you boys but I'm ready to give it my best if'n that's what ya hankering for.'

'Listen up. There's bin some changes around here, Jardine,' Sharky informed the still-arrogant Barton. 'Mighty big'uns.'

Barton rested his hands on his hips and suddenly realized that the two things he had not been furnished with after he had scrubbed the filth from his body and changed into fresh trail gear, were a gun and belt. His eyes darted at the gunbelt strapped around Sharky's middle. Both gun grips were poised for action.

Barton swallowed hard and defiantly edged towards the brutal Sharky. He was not a man to back down even when he knew the man he faced was far better with his hoglegs than he himself.

'What kinda changes ya talking about, Sharky?'

'I'm the new boss of the gang.'

Barton gasped. The words had hit him like a hammer. He was truly shocked by the unexpected statement. 'I got me a feeling ya ain't joshing with me. Are ya serious?'

'Dead serious, Jardine.' Sharky dropped one hand until it rested on the grip of one of his holstered guns. He stroked the notches carved into its grip. 'Me and the boys had us a vote and I won. I'm the new leader.'

The startled Barton glanced around the faces of the other men. Those faces were all smiling back at him. He then returned his attention to Sharky and waved a fist at the outlaw.

'Ya can't do this, Sharky. This is my gang. My gang. I'm the only one who can take us to Whispering Skull. Without me ya ain't ever gonna lay hands on the treasure there. I had me some time to figure out our next job when I was stuck in that cell back at Fort Addams and I reckon that when we've done that we'll head on to Whispering Skull.'

'Ain't no more jobs,' Sharky drawled.

'What?'

'Ya heard me. We're heading to Whispering Skull *now*.' Sharky spat a line of smoke at Barton. It curled around the man like a shroud.

'We do the job first,' Barton insisted. 'This is still my gang. Without me ya nothing. I made ya the most feared gang in a half-dozen territories. This is my gang.'

'It was your gang,' Sharky conceded. 'It sure ain't now.'

Barton moved around the area where men and horses stood shoulder to shoulder, vainly seeking support. There was none to be found from any of the other five outlaws. All they had were the sickly smiles of men ready to wager on a cockfight. Barton was utterly bewildered. He stopped and looked straight into Sharky's eyes.

'What ya come and rescue me for if I ain't the boss no more, Sharky?' he raged. 'Ya could have left me there to have my neck snapped. Why did ya save me?'

'We saved ya coz ya knows something we want to know, Jardine,' Sharky answered through a line of smoke. 'How to get to Whispering Skull and rustle up the treasure ya say is there. Savvy?'

'Ya mean ya was willing to risk being killed just to be led to Whispering Skull?' Barton snarled, then grinned. 'That's right. None of ya knows where it is. Without me none of ya will ever find it. Reckon I oughta just keep that information to myself.'

'We reckoned on ya saying that,' Elam said.

'Sharky said if ya don't take us there now we'll just have to kill ya like the worthless dog ya are.' Tey Tyler chuckled.

Barton stepped closer to Sharky. 'Like I said, without me ya ain't ever gonna find it.'

Sharky made a fist and brought it up swiftly. His gloved knuckles skidded across Barton's jaw. The sound of cracking teeth filled the desolate area as the stunned outlaw went cartwheeling backwards. Barton lay in the sand for a few moments, staring at the guns that surrounded him. Guns with hands curled around them in readiness. He shook his head, spat blood, then slowly he rose to his feet again.

'Kill me,' Barton snarled like a rabid wolf. 'You'll never find that treasure without me.'

'Me and the boys are plumb sick of ya telling us about that place and never ever taking us there,' Sharky said. He sucked even harder on his cigar. 'We figured we'd give ya a chance to take us there now. Otherwise ya gonna die. Die slow. I figure we could empty our guns into ya without killing ya, Jardine. A bullet in the knee and then one in the belly and so on. Gonna be begging us to finish ya off by the time we empty our .45s into every worthless part of that carcass of yours. Think about it.'

Barton thought about it.'

It was not a pleasant thought. Sometimes a swift death was a far better option than a lingering slow one. Barton looked at them all in turn but knew there was no mercy in any of their blackened souls. He returned his eyes to Sharky as blood trickled down his jaw.

'Humour me, Sharky. Why'd ya ask me if I feel lucky?'

Sharky Cole sucked in smoke and grinned.

'Well, put it this way, *amigo*. Ya lucky me and the boys sprung ya. Ya also gonna be mighty lucky if ya takes us to Whispering Skull right now. But luck comes in two kinds. Good and bad. Well? Which'll it be?'

Elroy Elam stepped forward. 'Do ya feel lucky, Jardine?'

The others roared with laughter.

Jardine Barton stopped talking at last. He ran his sleeve across his bloody mouth and sighed heavily.

'Only a fool would choose bad luck. I'll take ya.'

Sharky thrust a finger into Barton's chest and knocked him backwards into the arms of the others. 'Now ya being smart, Jardine. Take us there and you'll be as rich as the rest of us.'

Barton forced himself free of the outlaws. He stumbled to the side of his horse and held on to its reins as his mind raced. He swallowed hard. The taste of the blood lingered.

Jardine Barton glanced at the six outlaws. A chill traced up his spine. All he had to do was to take them to Whispering Skull.

The trouble was, he had been lying to them for years. There was no such place as Whispering Skull as far as he knew. No place where a treasure lay waiting to be harvested.

A single lie had grown like a cancer into a whole pack of lies.

Each embellishment had added something even more tempting to the men he had once controlled. Now his bluff had been called.

Sharky patted Barton on the back.

'I knew ya would see sense,' the outlaw grunted as the rest of the men walked off to water and feed their horses. 'Soon we'll be rich, Jardine. Then we can hightail it to California and live like kings for the rest of our days.'

'Reckon so,' Barton said, blood dripping from his lips.

The chilling realization engulfed Barton. He knew that all he had to do to remain alive was lead the gang of bloodthirsty outlaws to a place called Whispering Skull.

A mythical place which was somewhere west of his wildest imaginings.

Easy.

5

The fading light was unnerving. The crimson ripples of rays that spread across the heavens did nothing to ease the fear which still gripped the innards of the terrified cowboy as he kept spurring his exhausted quarter horse in an attempt to escape this unholy place. Jeff Stewart had been scared when he had first heard the distant sound of gunfire but when the massive explosion had sent black clouds laden with debris up into an otherwise cloudless sky his heart had almost broken loose from his chest. No matter how he rode, he could still hear those shots and gun-powder blasts inside his mind. There were badmen in these canyons and he knew that he was no match for that breed. Perhaps if he had a hand-tooled shooting rig strapped around his hips with a pair of pearl-handled Peacemakers sitting in well-oiled holsters he might not have been afraid, he thought, as the well-trained horse kept negotiating the stony ground beneath its hoofs. But then he noticed the first of the stars in the early-night sky and another rush of terror gripped his very soul.

He was used to sleeping beneath the stars and had never thought anything of it. As long as you had a mighty-well-fed campfire to nestle up against, the critters always kept their distance and let a man sleep. But there would be no campfire this night, nor perhaps on any of those that followed. A fire might keep wild cats and wolves at bay but it was a lure to two-legged badmen in search of fresh prey. He jabbed his spurs again and kept the horse moving as he glanced over his shoulder down the length of the canyon he now found himself in.

He could see nothing along the twisting canyon. No hint of anyone on his trail. He looked ahead again. Where was he? When would this maze of rocks end and allow him to find a green range once more?

The horse was flagging just like its master, yet his terror drove the spurs into its flanks over and over again.

'Keep goin', boy. Keep goin',' Stewart almost pleaded with the animal that he knew might drop at any moment. He was a cowboy and normally never made a horse suffer. Now it was different. In his mind's ear he could still hear echoes of the massive explosion that had shaken the very ground under him.

His eyes searched the ragged rocks on both sides. He still could not understand how he had managed to find himself in this territory. He had left fertile grassland behind him and thought if he just aimed the nose of his mount south he would find even lusher ranges and a new job. But heading south was the wrong thing to have done. It had led to this devilish landscape: a land where the bleached bones of those who had travelled here before him lay scattered all around.

'I should have headed east or west,' he mumbled to himself. 'There are mountains with trees on them there. Why ain't there no damn trees here?'

The redness in the sky was fading fast. More and more stars were sparkling against the black velvet heavens. The darker it became the more fearful he grew. Scared was one thing but being terrified was something totally new to the cowboy. The youngster had never been troubled when trying to break the spirit of a bucking bronco but the thought of meeting up with hardened gunfighters chilled him to the bone.

He whipped the shoulders of the dapple-grey with the tails of his rein leathers and the horse once again somehow found another burst of pace. The sight of the twisting plume of black smoke rising up from somewhere beyond the lake of white salt was still branded into his every thought. He did not know that the smoke he had seen was rising from a prison after it had been attacked and virtually destroyed by the Barton gang. All the cowboy knew for sure was that someone had blown something up.

Something big.

Mighty big.

Good folks did not tend to do that sort of thing. Not in his world anyway. Whoever it had been who had set flame to powder were probably the same people who had been firing their guns a short while before.

Jeff Stewart wanted nothing more than to escape before he too became another notch on the grip of a gunslinger's gun. Yet how did you escape from a land which seemed to have become a maze of twisting canyons and draws set between massive high-shouldered mountains of rock?

He eased back on his reins as another equally frightening thought occurred to him.

Spurring the horse on might in fact be forcing it into the jaws of those you were trying to avoid. He had lost all sense of which direction he was heading in. For all he knew he might have gone in a huge circle through the twisting canyons and was actually driving his mount right back to where they had first heard the gunplay.

His heart sank.

He might be riding right towards the very men he was trying to flee from. He slowed the grey to a walk and tried to listen out for sounds which might give him some answers.

What if they were ahead?

Stewart swung round on his saddle.

Fear was strangling him.

Where were they now? The shooting had long stopped but the echoes remained in his youthful mind. The shadows had started to creep and grow all around his lathered-up mount. The black jagged shadows traced across the trail ahead of him until everything changed shape in the rider's tired mind.

It had been a couple of hours since the ground beneath his dapple-grey's hoofs had shaken yet Stewart's heart was still galloping even if his weary mount was down to a walk. A million questions had raced through his fertile imagination and the naive horseman did not have a single answer for any of them. All he knew was that there was trouble in the mountainous region of pink sandstone monuments, and it was close.

The horse needed feed and water but the terror which filled Stewart's every fibre refused to allow either of them to rest for even a second. He wanted to escape this strange land and find somewhere he was more used to. A blade of green grass or a tree with leaves upon its branches might have calmed the cowboy, but no matter how far he rode, there was nothing except the same mocking sandstone-coloured walls of rock. Not even cactus seemed able to grow here, he thought. No tumbleweed or purple sage clumps could exist in this strange territory.

As he thought about it he realized he

had not seen anything which looked alive for over two weeks. A chill raced through his young aching body. It was not the drop in temperature but the fact that he now knew he had made the biggest mistake of his short life. One which might put an end to it permanently.

'Should have stayed north,' Stewart said as he kept looking for something which might raise his spirits. If there was anything here capable of doing that he sure could not see it.

Everything seemed to be dead, the cowboy reasoned. No matter how far he urged the grey on, he found nothing which gave even a hint of life. He needed hope. Hope of there being something ahead which was better than everything he had left behind him since he had heard the gunfire.

After what had seemed like an eternity the sun was dropping behind the jagged peaks that surrounded Stewart as he kept trying to put distance between himself and the mysterious people who, he knew, were also travelling through this perilous land.

The cowboy kept teasing his reins to encourage the slow-walking horse onward. He stood in his stirrups and took another long lingering look at the landscape before the sunlight finally vanished.

He wondered. Could the darkness save him?

Save him from becoming another dead man in a land which was filled with the white bones of so many other dead things?

Was the darkness going to help him find a way out of the maze of canyons, or would it just hinder his attempts to see the trail away from this devilish place? The question haunted him. There had to be a trail which led back to normal land, didn't there?

Perhaps this was not just another real land at all, he thought. Maybe it was something else. Maybe he had some-how ridden straight into Hell itself. He rubbed the tails of his bandanna across his face. But you had to be dead to end up in Hell.

Stewart bit his lip.

'Holy smoke. I might be dead and too dumb to know it.'

The sky darkened. Now there were just stars above them.

Stewart kept his horse moving. He noticed there was no moon in the heavens far above, just thousands of stars filling the vast expanse of black. Darkness could be his saviour, or it might just be the end of him, he thought. A merciless sun had burned him until his skin had started to flake off his face and now he could feel it getting colder. Was Hell now going to reverse its torture and freeze him to death instead?

He was trapped within a nightmare.

The sudden drop in temperature was like a straight razor to Stewart's senses. It hurt as he hauled his trusty jacket off his cantle and put it on over his dust-laden shirt.

Thirst was the only thing that reminded him that he was still alive. His throat hurt. It had been a long ride since he had last managed to fill his canteens.

The young cowboy wondered if the coming of night might help him avoid the men he knew were out there someplace. The lack of a moon might allow him to escape the eyes of gunmen he feared.

The trouble was it also made the unfamiliar terrain even more daunting. One false move and he knew his horse might throw a shoe and become lame. This was not a place to be without a horse.

The horse was now barely moving.

How long would it be before he found a place that resembled something he was used to? A thousand questions raced through his weary mind as he kept the horse moving ever onward into the depths of a canyon bathed in blackness.

The dapple-grey was starting to sway

beneath him. The cowboy knew that in normal circumstances he would never have made the pitiful animal go for so long without rest. The horse started to snort as if it were ready to drop.

'Easy, boy.' Stewart eased back on his reins and stopped the horse. He looped his right leg over the neck of the grey, slid to the ground and held tightly on to its bridle. 'Reckon it's time for me to walk.'

The searching eyes of the cow-puncher looked all about him and tried to see into the shadows, which were even blacker than the rest of the canyon. He inhaled deeply. The air was cold and frosty in his lungs. He could hear the rocks which surrounded him crackle as the day's heat escaped and rose towards the stars.

'Gotta find us some water, boy,' the cowboy said, trying vainly to forget about the shots and the explosions that had terrified him earlier. 'C'mon.'

The horseman led the grey deeper into the shadows. For more than an hour they walked through the twisting canyon, master and mount in search of the one thing they knew was mighty scarce in this unholy place. Each step took them further and further away from the vast lake of crystal salt and deeper into the labyrinth of perilous spires that loomed over them like something created in the minds of the insane.

The cowboy stopped and felt the nose of his faithful horse resting against the pit of his spine. He looked down at his boots. Boots he could barely see in the blackness that engulfed them. His feet hurt. Each high-sided boot was filled with sweat or blood or both. The worn leather inside the boots cut into his feet like shards of broken glass. Like all cowboys he wore high-heeled boots ideal for balancing in stirrups but not meant for walking in. Especially across rugged ground.

'We're in trouble, boy,' Stewart admitted to his trusty horse as it snorted against his back. 'I sure done put us in a real bad pickle this time and no mistake.'

The sweat-lathered grey lowered its head as its master dropped to the ground and sat on rocks that neither of them could see clearly in the dark shadows.

'If'n I hadn't have bin so feared of getting shot up we sure wouldn't have ended in this mess.' Stewart sighed as the fingers of his free hand fumbled in the breast pockets of his coat for his tobacco pouch. He found the small bag and brought it close to his face. His eyes had not adjusted as they normally did after sundown. It was as though this darkness was different somehow from any that he had ever travelled through before. He dropped his reins and the quarter horse did not move a muscle.

Stewart sprinkled the makings along the gummed paper, rolled it into a crude cigarette, then tugged the draw-string of the tobacco pouch tight with his teeth. The pouch dangled from his mouth as his gloved fingers managed to roll the paper around its filling. His tongue then slid drily along the gummed edge to complete the task.

'Reckon we're done for,' Stewart sighed.

The horse suddenly snorted and raised its head in a jerking fashion. Stewart gazed up at the animal curiously.

'Ya heard something, boy?' the cowboy asked, putting the pouch back in his breast pocket. Suddenly he began to think about where they were. In a remote canyon shrouded in darkness. 'What ya heard? A cougar or something? Ain't sure what kinda critters this hell-hole might be hiding.'

The grey dragged a hoof across the ground. Fearfully Stewart got back to his feet and placed the cigarette in the corner of his dry mouth. The horse snorted violently and shook its head. Its mane caught the wisps of faint starlight as its master took hold of the loose reins.

'What's wrong?' Stewart knew that

73

horses were far quicker when it came to hearing and smelling things that men tended not to notice. The horse was looking straight ahead of them. The cowboy vainly tried to see what had caught the attention of the alert gelding. It was impossible. Whatever it was, it was a mystery to the cowpuncher. 'Reckon it can't be nothing dangerous or you'd be backing off or hightailing it. Right, boy? So what in tarnation are ya looking at? What?'

The horse snorted and started to walk forward. Stewart remained at its shoulder, holding on to the reins in case the animal bolted away. For what felt like a lifetime the pair kept staggering along the black canyon. Then the horse started to nod over and over again and move its muscular frame with more purpose. Whatever was out there, the dapple-grey wanted to get to it as quickly as it could.

The cowboy could feel the reins being pulled free of his gloved hands as the animal started to increase its pace.

The shadows were blacker than anything either of them had walked though before but the grey was unafraid. It kept pulling away from its weary master until Stewart felt the reins tugged from his grip. The gelding suddenly began to trot. The sound of its hoofs echoed all around the cowboy as, ignoring the pain of his aching, blistered feet he ran after his mount.

The cowboy had to run for more than 200 yards before he caught sight of the now stationary grey horse's wide rump and black tail. The animal was close to the foot of the canyon wall.

Stewart was confused.

'What ya run off for like that?' He slowed up as he reached the horse, then realized what had drawn his faithful mount like a moth to a naked flame.

Water.

If his horse had not been making so much noise drinking from the pool Stewart might not have even noticed it. The cowboy stopped to get his second wind and then saw the rippling of starlight dancing on the surface of the small pool of water. It sparkled like diamonds, but this was far more precious than diamonds.

'Water!' Stewart gasped thankfully. He walked towards it and tried to control his emotions. He patted the shoulder of the still-drinking horse, then pulled all of his empty canteens from the saddle horn and began to unscrew the stopper of the first. 'Ya might not know it, boy, but ya saved my bacon.'

A bitter taste filled his mouth. Stewart realized that he was still chewing on his unlit cigarette. Most of its makings had fallen free of the rolled paper whilst the remainder filled his arid mouth. Stewart no longer wanted to fill his lungs with smoke. Now all he wanted to do was to fill his belly with water. He pulled the twisted paper from his lips, screwed it up, tossed it away and waited.

He would wait until his horse had drunk its fill before he would drop his canteens into the dark liquid.

'I sure hope this ain't the last water we find before we reaches civilization,' Stewart said with a sigh. 'If'n we ever do find a way out of this damned place.'

Then he suddenly heard a distant sound.

A cruelly haunting sound which he recognized.

Stewart felt the hairs on the nape of his neck rise in alarmed warning. He took a step away from the horse and listened hard. Then heard the sound again.

It was the sound of wagon chains and horses' hoofs echoing off the high canyon walls. A lot of horses' hoofs. With each beat of his racing heart the noise grew louder. It had to be the men who had been shooting earlier, he told himself.

The same varmints who had sent clouds of smoke into the otherwise pristine heavens when they had ignited their explosives.

They were getting closer.

A cold shiver swept through the cowboy.

'Damn it all. It's them,' he whispered to himself as a sickening realization dawned upon him. 'And they're headed right here. Holy smoke. Them varmints are headed for this very place.'

Stewart cautiously ventured a few more steps away from his horse and screwed up his sore eyes. He stared down through the long twisting canyon into the blackness. Dark as the canyon was, he could see movement amid the shadows. Terror raced through him again. A terror which was even greater than the one which had chilled him to the bone earlier that day.

It must be same men who had been firing their shooting irons back towards the lake of crystal salt. The same men who had then resorted to using gunpowder a short while later.

Who else would be travelling through this godforsaken land of the dead?

He knew he was right.

They were coming as surely as night

followed day. Slowly but surely they were heading along the very same canyon as he and his mount had ridden through for the last few hours. A desperation swept through the cowboy.

'Of all the damn trails they could have taken, them varmints chose the same'un as I did. Why?' Stewart snorted.

It was hard to be accurate but as far as Stewart could tell they were still a couple of miles away from where he stood. Then his tired eyes spotted something he had not expected. A fiery torch that swayed as though it were attached to the top of a wagon hoop danced in the darkness. Its flickering light seemed to be waving at the solitary onlooker. His heart sank. This was no delusion brought on by lack of water or sheer exhaustion, this was real.

'Gotta hide someplace.' Stewart looked all around him for somewhere to conceal himself and his mount. There was none. The towering jagged canyon walls had him trapped on both sides.

There was only one way to avoid them.

He had to go deeper into the merciless canyon. If he wanted to escape them he had to keep going into the depths of the maze of deadly unforgiving canyons and pray that he might find a way out of this nightmare before the riders caught up with him.

Would it lead him to safetly?

Stewart doubted it.

He spun on his heels, ran back to the small pool of water, dropped on to his knees and submerged his canteens into the black liquid. With bubbles rising around his wrists he looked out into the dark shadows.

The torch was still coming towards him.

The terrifying sound of the riders' wagon chains and horses' hoofs grew ever louder. The cowboy looked down at the canteens as his horse raised its head. Bubbles kept on rising around both his hands. Again he returned his eyes to the approaching men. Men he could not see but could sense.

'Fill up, damn it,' Stewart snarled at the canteens. 'We ain't got time to linger. We gotta hightail it pretty damn soon.'

6

Thousands of stars shone like diamonds over the arid terrain, which led down to where Fort Addams lay in ruins amid the shadowy rocks. But there was something else cast against the magnificent night sky. It was a thin trail of smoke rising into the heavens from fires that refused to go out. Even in the middle of the long cold night the embers of the smouldering prison could be clearly seen by the approaching army patrol. As the horsemen cut down through a frosty draw towards their destination each of them in turn could see where the smoke was originating from.

A flickering red glow seemed to be gently massaging the stars hanging in the black sky as smoke still trailed upward from the remnants of the once proud prison. What was left of Fort

Addams was sending out a pitiful message to anyone who might be able to see its final gasps for salvation. The wailing of the trapped prisoners had ceased hours earlier as one by one they sank on to the floors of their cells and waited for death to come for them as it had come for all of their guards.

Death had already captured the souls of their captors but each of the prisoners knew his own death would take far longer to bring oblivion.

Apart from the last of the flames, which still managed to crawl through the rubble, the remote prison was eerily silent.

The score of troopers drew rein behind their broad-shouldered captain as the officer raised himself high in his stirrups and stared in disbelief through the gloom at what was left of Fort Addams. Captain Jerome Hyde fell back on to his saddle and then glanced at the face of his sergeant. The crimson glow danced across the solid features of the burly man.

'Am I having a hallucination, Riley?' Hyde asked, tightening his white gauntlets over his hands.

'I ain't sure what one of them is exactly, Captain,' Riley responded honestly, as he too tried to comprehend the sight before them. 'But if it's seeing a whole mess of rubble where there oughta be a prison, then ya are.'

Captain Hyde inhaled deeply. The scent of burning flesh filled his nostrils.

'We'd better head on in.'

'Well, there ain't no damn walls to stop us.' Riley nodded.

The officer raised an arm and called out,

'Troopers advance.'

As Hyde's white gauntlet was lowered the reluctant riders slowly began to follow their leader. Apart from the bugler they were all raw recruits. All fresh-faced and innocent.

Sergeant Riley tapped his spurs and turned to face the riders behind them. He bellowed out, 'C'mon ya sorrowful bunch of egg-suckers. Ain't nothing to be afraid of. Whoever done this is long gone by now.'

The cavalry steered their mounts through the rocks towards the shattered walls of the prison. Hyde kept his skittish charger in check as it too caught the acrid stench of death on the night air.

'Keep a firm grip on your reins, men,' Captain Hyde called out. 'Horses don't like this sort of thing.'

Even the faint light of the stars could not disguise the horror that faced them as they rode into the courtyard. Debris and parts of bodies were strewn everywhere. The flames still licked up through what was left of the buildings ahead of them as they advanced.

'What could have happened?' Hyde asked out loud as they passed the supply wagons. 'Maybe the arsenal exploded. Do you think that's what happened, Riley?'

The experienced eyes of the sergeant darted all around them as the prisoners started to awaken and call out at the unexpected visitors.

'Well, Riley?' Hyde raised his voice. 'Do you think the arsenal blew up and did this terrible thing?'

Riley dragged his reins back and steadied his horse. 'Nope.'

Hyde heeled his own mount round in a circle, then eased back on his reins. He looked hard at the man with the broken nose.

'You don't?'

'Nope,' Riley repeated.

The rest of the troopers stopped their horses behind them.

'Then what?' Hyde pressed.

'This was no accident, Captain,' Riley sighed. 'This was done by a bunch of critters no better than them prisoners yonder. This was deliberate killing.'

Hyde swung his horse around and tried to see whatever it was his sergeant had seen. No matter how hard he tried he could see nothing but death and destruction.

'How can you be so positive?'

Riley eased himself down from his horse, kept hold of his reins in his powerful hands, sniffed at the air and then looked up into Hyde's face.

'Can ya smell that?'

'I can smell burning flesh,' Hyde answered.

'Not that.' Riley sniffed loudly. 'Can ya smell it.'

'Smell what, Sergeant?'

'Black powder,' Riley replied. 'This was done with black powder. The smell of that stuff hangs around for days.'

The captain sniffed the air once more. Then he too caught the scent of gunpowder in his nostrils. 'Damn it. I think you might be right, Riley.'

'And there weren't no black powder stored in the arsenal here, Captain,' Riley said. 'Bullets for carbines and pistols, but no black powder.'

'So whoever did this brought barrels of gunpowder with them,' Hyde muttered slowly. 'They must have been concealed in one of the wagons.'

Riley pointed the tips of his reins

ahead of them. 'There was a wagon over there by the arsenal. That's the one which had the powder in it, Captain.'

Hyde dismounted and stood next to his sergeant. 'How can you tell there was a wagon there?'

'Look at the ground,' Riley growled. 'Ya can still see the wagon grooves in the sand. They leads right up to where that big black hole in the ground is.'

'You're right.' Hyde ran a gloved finger across his lips. The prisoners' cries grew louder.

Riley waved at the troopers, then pointed at the caged prisoners. 'Dismount and go water them noisy egg-suckers yonder.'

Hyde kicked at the ground.

'Whoever did this, Riley, they must have wanted to free someone real bad.'

'Someone mighty bad by my reckoning, Captain.' The sergeant repeated the words and then chuckled.

The officer looked at Riley. 'I see no humour in any of this, Riley.'

The stalwart sergeant stared out at

the mountains bathed in eerie starlight, then tilted his head to look at the annoyed officer.

'I sure do. By the looks of the hoof tracks they all headed south, Captain. That's darn funny.'

'Why?'

'Only a locobean would head that-away, Captain,' Riley replied. 'Apart from a lake of solid salt there ain't nothing for a hundred miles except fallen-down mountains. Some folks say there's a trail through them rocks but they're usually folks with fried brains. Nope. Whoever bust the prisoner loose from here sure ain't done the varmint no favours. The Shoshoni calls that place the land of the dead.'

'Land of the dead?'

'Yep.'

Hyde watched the sergeant lead his mount towards one of the few water troughs still intact. The officer gathered up his own reins and followed.

7

It grew even darker along the rugged gorge as the cowboy steered his mount higher and higher up into the rocks in the hope of finding a path out of the canyon and away from the men behind him. The trail was wide and yet perilous. It clung to the side of the rockface and seemed to head on up towards the very stars. A million years earlier it had probably been a path where a river of molten lava flowed but the cowboy knew nothing of such things. All he knew was that he had found a trail which might lead him to a place of sanctuary. A place where he could either hide or find a way out of the devilish land he was trapped in.

Exhausted, Jeff Stewart pulled the horse to a stop and stared down. It seemed as if he were sitting on top of the world and yet he was less than halfway up the strange mountain. There had to be a way out of here and away from those who followed, he kept telling himself.

If there had been a moon he might have been able to see a way to escape, he thought. On the other hand, a moon might have made him an easy target. The moon could be a good friend but it could also be a bad enemy.

The cowboy toyed with his reins and looked down. Down into a lake of nothing but blackness. It was even darker below him than it was in the ragged group of rocks through which he had found himself navigating. The trail sloped to the very edge of the rockface. The horse dropped its head and the cowboy slid from his saddle on to the uneven ground. He could feel every sharp rock beneath his boot leather. Stewart held the reins tightly and mopped the sweat from his face with his bandanna tails as he studied the trail which faced his burning eyes.

The moonless sky made it impossible

to make out anything in detail as clouds drifted across the stars. If there was a way over the cliffs which loomed above him the cowpuncher could not see it. He turned and looked down into the blackness again.

A blackness which was everywhere, and it was getting darker. More and more stars were being blotted out as clouds floated across their heavenly light. He felt sick and knew he needed food or sleep but there was no time to sleep or eat.

No time to rest.

No time to do anything except await a bullet from an unseen rifle. He bit his lip and kept firm hold of his mount as he checked the tired animal over for injuries. Somehow the horse was not lame. Somehow it had managed to do everything its master had commanded of it.

'Reckon I'll walk ya for a while,' Stewart told the horse. Carefully he moved to the nose of the animal and gripped its bridle in his gloved hand.

Then, just as he was about to turn to face the upward trail again, his heart sank. He stopped and stared down into the blackness at the fiery torch he could see, less than a quarter mile behind and below him.

Stewart screwed up his eyes and forced them to focus on everything around the illumination of the blazing torch. For a while he could not make out anything clearly; then it all became all too clear. He could see the riders around the slowly moving wagon in the flickering light of the torch, which was tied to one of the metal hoops which arched over the vehicle's flatbed. The canvas of the wagon was pulled halfway back over the wagon, exposing the outlaws' provisions. A man was perched on the driver's board, steering as the others flanked the vehicle on both sides.

The cowboy rested a hand on the rocks beside him and leaned away from his mount to get a better view. Then he saw the rifles in the hands of the horsemen. Each wooden stock was resting on the thigh of a rider, its metal barrel aimed heavenward.

For the first time Stewart could see them.

See the men he feared.

'Holy smoke!' The cowboy heaved a sigh as he straightened up and rubbed his lips with his gloved fingers. 'They look a real mean bunch of critters. Even worse than I had figured. I sure don't wanna tangle with any of them.'

He looked all around him and wondered whether they would keep travelling along the floor of the canyon below his high vantage point. Keep travelling on to wherever they were headed without ever knowing that their passing had been witnessed. If they did pass below him and kept on going Stewart knew that he could retrace his tracks and head off in the opposite direction.

Without even realizing it, Stewart started to smile.

Within a few moments they would pass beneath him, he told himself. Pass and never have a clue as to his existence.

'Reckon we might just stay living until sun-up, boy,' he told the dapple-grey. 'Them dumb guntoting riders ain't got no idea that we're up here watching them. Ain't that a joke and . . .'

His words faded as inside his chest Stewart felt his heart quicken once again. He moved down the length of his horse and stared back along the trail up which he had ridden. They too had discovered the trail.

'No. Can't be,' Stewart gasped.

To his utter surprise and horror the cowboy watched the torchlight move from the centre of the canyon as the wagon and its outriders aimed for the very same trail that he himself had taken earlier.

The cowboy forced his knuckles against his teeth and stood in wide-eyed terror as the wagon and the horsemen started up the trail to where he stood watching.

There was no mistake. No error. The wagon and its guardians were heading up the steep mountain trail towards him. The flutters of night breeze caught the flames of the torch, sending its light dancing up the metal shafts of their Winchester barrels. The cowboy knew he was in trouble. Big trouble.

'Oh sweet Lord. They're coming up here,' Stewart gasped in disbelief. His mind raced as he grabbed his saddle horn, threw his aching body back on to his saddle and rammed his boot toes into his stirrups. In desperation he looked ahead of him but saw nothing but blackness. 'Sorry, boy. We gotta ride.'

The cowboy spurred.

Somehow the dapple-grey obeyed.

* * *

Less than an hour had passed but to the troopers amongst the wreckage of what had once been regarded as the finest prison in the West it felt as though they had only just arrived. None of the twenty-one cavalrymen knew who had managed to destroy Fort Addams and had left the prisoners either to starve to death or die a lingering death from thirst in their cramped stinking cells, but whoever it was they were an awesome adversary. Since their arrival Captain Hyde had brooded on how many men had actually attacked the remote prison. From what remained of Fort Addams it appeared that an army had besieged it, but he knew that that was impossible. Lack of numbers had been made up for with well-placed explosives and a cunning, daringly executed plan. This was like looking into a henhouse and seeing what a solitary fox could achieve.

The seasoned cavalry officer was well used to bloodshed, but he, like so many of his contemporaries, had been sent West after the war. Hyde was used to facing fellow soldiers where even the most gruesome of battles followed mutually acknowledged rules, but since he had found himself in the West he had realized that there were no rules beyond the Pecos river. Men out here killed for the sheer joy of killing and not for the greater good.

There was a tension within the shattered walls of the prison which filtered down from Captain Hyde to the younger men. Even the raw recruits who had barely been in the army long enough for the ink to have dried on their enlistment papers felt uneasy at the prospect of encountering anyone who was capable of pulling off such a feat. Yet each of them knew that that might be exactly what would be expected of them should their leader decide to follow the hoof tracks found by Sergeant Riley.

Each of the weary troopers eyed the figure of Jerome Hyde as he paced around the destruction over and over again.

Hyde was a man who had earned his rank and a chestful of ribbons the hard way. He had come up through the ranks and ridden shoulder to shoulder with George Armstrong Custer during the long bitter war. Unlike Custer though, Hyde had not been headstrong and flamboyant. He had always acted with measured thought, not only for his men but also for his enemies. He had not simply charged into the thick of it with his sabre held high like Custer. He had never willingly risked either his own life or those of his men. Hyde had always tried to consider his options. Like all great leaders of men he wanted to win by taking the least amount of risk.

Until now.

Now there was a storm brewing inside him. Perhaps it was the stench of rotting flesh which was fuelling his anger, but for the very first time in his military career he wanted to act without due consideration. He wanted to avenge the men who had been massacred in Fort Addams.

In all the years he had fought during the war he had never seen anything

99

quite as evil as the devastation which surrounded him in the charred rubble that had, until only hours earlier, been a massive fortress.

Whoever had done this terrible thing was utterly merciless, he thought. Again the officer wondered which prisoner might have been able to muster the dregs of humanity to come and effect his escape.

Hyde paused by the huge crater in the ground where flesh still clung to the sides of the smoking hole. It might have been the middle of the night but he could hear flies battling over the melted morsels of what had once been men and animals. It sickened the experienced officer as the burly sergeant ambled back towards him. Hyde gave a nod of recognition.

'Riley,' he muttered.

'The men have fed and watered the prisoners, Captain,' Riley said in a long-drawn-out sigh. 'I got a few of them to bury the bodies of those guards we could recognize as being men, sir.

They also threw the scatterings in with the bodies.'

Hyde glanced at the large man. 'Scatterings?'

Riley pulled out a corncob pipe and blew down its stem.

'Yep. Scatterings. You know, the legs and things that was scattered all over.'

The officer nodded and clapped his hands together behind his back. 'Of course. Scatterings. A strange but quite accurate word for them. It'll take a whole lot longer for anyone to find enough to bury in that rubble, Riley.'

'Reckon it ain't even worth trying, sir.'

'Reluctantly I am forced to agree.'

'We headed back to Fort Lincoln after sun-up, Captain?' Riley asked. He started to fill his pipe bowl with tobacco from his pouch as he watched the troubled officer begin pacing once again. Riley followed.

Hyde looked at his sergeant. 'Impossible.'

'How come?' Riley asked.

'We cannot just go back to Lincoln, Sergeant,' Hyde muttered. 'We have dozens of prisoners here who have to be fed and watered until the authorities decide what has to be done with them. We can't desert them and leave them to die of thirst or starvation. That's what the bastards who destroyed the fort did, Riley. Those caged prisoners might be scum but they do not deserve to be abandoned by United States cavalry-men.'

Riley poked the tobacco into the pipe bowl with his thumb and looked across at the gallows that had been built at the furthest end of the courtyard. It had survived the explosions, unlike the adobe walls.

'OK. We could leave a handful of men here to tend the prisoners. Then the rest of us could go on back to Lincoln and tell the commanding officer what's happened.' Riley placed the stem of his pipe between his teeth. 'Then it'd be up to the authorities to figure out what to do with them.'

Hyde did not reply for a moment. 'What about the ruthless men who did this, Sergeant? They cannot be allowed to ride away from this scot free. They have to be brought to book.'

'I'd let the elements deal with 'em, sir,' Riley said.

'This was mass murder,' Hyde retorted. 'I intend making each and every one of those involved in this pay. Pay with their lives.'

'Like I told ya, Captain. Them varmints is as good as dead already.' Riley repeated his earlier statement. 'They've ridden into the land of the dead. I don't give them any chance of surviving, sir. They'll be buzzard-bait within a week.'

'But what if they do survive, Riley,' Hyde persisted.

Riley struck a match along his pants, cupped its flame over the pipe bowl and sucked. Smoke billowed around the sergeant's head.

'I surely doubt anyone can survive in them mountains and canyons, sir.'

'But the point is, they might.' Hyde started to pace again to where two of the troopers were tending their horses. 'They might live to brag about what they have done. Brag at how they not only freed a prisoner but destroyed an entire prison and killed every one of the guards within its walls. No. I cannot allow that to happen.'

Trailing smoke in his wake like a locomotive Riley caught up with his superior. 'What ya mean, Captain? Are ya seriously figuring on following them locobeans out into them mountains yonder? That's suicide, sir.'

There was another pause as Hyde considered his words carefully before speaking again. 'It is not suicidal if you are well stocked-up on water and food. That place is only dangerous to the unprepared, Riley. We shall be prepared. There are still a lot of mules uninjured and harnessed to the last supply wagon. We can use them to carry extra water and provisions. I do not think the men we are going to hunt down will be so well furnished with the basics as we shall be.'

'I guess ya right,' Riley agreed with a shrug.

'I am right. We have to go after those evil bastards and bring them to justice. There is no other way. They have to be punished.'

'Them critters will surely put up a fight if'n we do manage to catch up with 'em,' Riley opined lugubriously. 'A mighty big fight if I'm any judge.'

Hyde sighed. 'We shall dish out justice from the barrels of our weaponry, Riley. There will probably be no other way.'

A wry smile etched the features of the sergeant. 'Ya mean we ain't gonna take us no prisoners, sir? Ya mean we can kill the galoots for what they done here?'

Hyde nodded.

The attention of the officer and his trusty sergeant was drawn to the approach of two of the troopers and a filthy prisoner in ankle shackles as they came across the starlit courtyard. The dishevelled prisoner was being urged on towards Hyde by the tips of their bayonets.

'What's going on here?' Riley boomed.

Both of the young soldiers kept the half-dead man moving until he reached Hyde and Riley.

'Reckon ya gotta hear what this critter bin telling us, Captain,' one of the young men said.

'He reckons he knows who done this and all,' the other trooper added.

Hyde stepped closer to the prisoner. He looked the man up and down before speaking.

'What have you to say?' he asked the prisoner.

The man, who stank from every pore of his rancid body, rubbed his face with his hands. 'Ya wanna know who them bastards freed, Captain? Do ya?'

Ignoring the sickening stench Hyde stepped closer. 'Speak.'

The prisoner tilted his head. 'What's in it for me?'

'What do you want?' Hyde raised his eyebrows.

Riley grabbed the man by the shoulder. 'Don't go messing with the officer or I'll break both ya legs.'

Hyde pushed Riley aside. 'Let the creature speak, Sergeant.'

'I want to be given a mule and let loose,' the man fearlessly replied. 'I wanna be able to live what's left of my days as a free man. Well?'

Riley gave a belly laugh. 'Ya sure ya don't want nothing else, little man? Maybe ya might hanker for a bucket of gold coin as well?'

'You must think your information is very valuable,' Hyde whispered to the man. 'Is it?'

The prisoner kept staring at Hyde. 'It sure is. I know who them killers sprung, Captain. I knows the name of the varmint they freed. That's gotta be worth something.'

'Tell me who they freed and I shall

consider what reward you will get,' Hyde said bluntly. 'Otherwise I shall have you horsewhipped.'

The prisoner thought for a moment, then nodded.

'Barton,' the man said. 'It was Jardine Barton.'

'Jardine Barton?' Hyde repeated the name as though he had just been poisoned. 'Are you sure?'

'Yep. It was his gang that done this OK. I recognized one of them. Sharky Cole. Ya see Barton was in that small cell in the yard, waiting to be hung. The gang rolled in on three wagons and then blew the place to bits. Then they done sprung Barton, washed him down and left the rest of us to die. Well? Is that worth anything, Captain?' The eyes of the prisoner danced in the torchlight. 'Is the news of who ya looking for worth anything?'

A stern-faced Hyde looked at the two young soldiers. 'Take this man back to his cell. Now.'

'Ya ain't no better than Barton,' the

prisoner shouted and spat angrily as the troopers hauled him round and started back towards the cells. 'I hope ya do tangle with him and his gang. They'll skin ya alive.'

Captain Hyde lowered his head. 'Give him extra rations.'

Riley kept puffing on his pipe as Hyde brooded. He then glanced at the prisoner as the half-dead creature shuffled back at the tips of the bayonets.

'By the face on ya I'd bet ya know this Barton critter.'

Hyde nodded. 'You might say I do, Riley.'

'Yeah?' Riley lifted his right leg and tapped the pipe against his boot. 'How?'

'How? Ten years ago, back East, long before the war, Jardine Barton killed my sister and half a dozen other innocent females when he robbed a bank.' Hyde rested a hand on a hitching rail beside one of the troughs. His eyes were gleaming with reflected sadness. 'I vowed that one day I would find and kill that animal for what he did to my innocent sister. After the war I tried to find out what had happened to Barton but there was nothing. Not even a newspaper article about him. I imagined he had probably died in the years I was away fighting. It never dawned on me that he had scurried away like a rat when the war had started out here, into the wastelands of one lawless territory after another to ply his evil trade.'

'A whole heap of yella-bellies run away from the war when it started, sir.' Riley sucked the last smoke from his pipe stem and spat at the ground. 'Ain't a whole lot of law out in these parts, and that suits some folks.'

Hyde opened his breast pocket and pulled out a gold timepiece. He snapped open the lid, revealing a faded photograph. The likeness did not do the female sitter justice, Hyde thought, but her beauty still lived in his mind's eye.

'Look at her, Riley,' the officer said

sadly. 'This is all there is to remind me. She was only fifteen and working as a bank teller. Barton cut her down just because he could. He killed everyone in that bank apart from a well-padded woman who somehow survived by the grace of her bone girdle.'

'Did she tell ya what happened?'

Hyde returned the gold watch back to his pocket and secured the silver button. 'Yes. She told me. She also told me how Barton had laughed after announcing his name to those trapped inside the bank. He laughed like a madman and then he started shooting.'

Riley pushed his pipe into his pocket and patted the back of his superior officer before walking back towards the rest of the troop.

'Reckon that changes things a tad.'

Hyde glanced at the larger man. 'Now I have a real reason to hunt those killers down. I will go alone if you feel it too dangerous, Sergeant.'

'I ain't feared of no woman-killer,' Riley growled. 'And I'll not let ya ride on ya lonesome, Captain. Hell, some-one gotta take care of ya.'

'Much obliged, Sergeant.'

'Always an honour to ride with ya, Captain.'

A thousand memories invaded the officer's thoughts as Hyde stared beyond the rubble and smoke out into the darkness where he knew the outlaws had fled. Like an eagle his narrowed eyes focused on the place his sergeant called the land of the dead. The black shapes of the craggy mountain range did not frighten him even though they did not resemble anything he had ever seen before and looked more like something from another world than anything he was used to.

'Jardine Barton,' he hissed like a sidewinder ready to strike. 'At long last I shall have the opportunity to make you pay for what you did to my dear Laura.'

8

Having seen the unknown horsemen take the same trail as he himself had chosen, the terrified Jeff Stewart had managed to urge the exhausted quarter horse a further hundred yards up the steep trail towards the crest of the rocky rise before the animal fell on to its knees beneath him. The cowboy crashed into the unforgiving ground and chewed on its dust before he managed to force himself back up on to his shaking legs. He moved to the snorting animal and knelt beside it. Expertly the cowboy checked the animal for injuries but found only a creature that had somehow managed to ride far beyond its normal endurance. Suds of sweat belied the cold air that surrounded them and fell in lumps from every part of the tired horse.

'Easy, boy. Try and get ya wind back,'

Stewart soothed. His eyes remained glued on the distant flame of the torch, which was still coming towards him.

Stewart rose and tried to think but his mind, like his muscles, was strained to the limit. He considered taking the saddle and gear off the back of the horse, but it was all he owned in the entire world. A cow-puncher was not going to get a lot of work without he had the basics, he told himself. He removed his hat and placed it in front of the horse's nose, then filled its bowl with an entire canteen of water.

'Drink, boy. Drink,' he told the faithful animal. The horse obeyed and soon emptied the contents of the upturned hat. 'That might get ya old bones oiled up a tad. I sure hope so, anyways.'

Stewart focused on the distant wagon and its out-riders. He felt sick in the pit of his guts. Who were they? What would they do if they spotted him? A bead of sweat trailed down from his limp hair as he replaced the Stetson back on his head. He felt he already knew the answers.

After a few moments which seemed to last an eternity the cowboy stood in front of his kneeling horse and grabbed both sides of its bridle. He shook it until the animal again gave out a mighty snort of disapproval.

'Now get back up on them legs, boy.' Stewart leaned back and tugged at the head of the horse. Again and again he repeated the action as he kept watching the riders bathed in torchlight come ever closer. 'C'mon, ya stubborn old fool. Ya wanna end up buzzard bait? Get up.'

Again the horse somehow managed to disregard its own agony and force itself up on to its unsteady hoofs. Stewart patted the neck of his mount heartily.

'Good, boy. Don't go fretting none, I ain't gonna get back in the saddle no more. Now I'll walk ya.'

The cowpuncher turned and looked to the very crest of the canyon wall where the blackness of the shadows seemed to allow the faintest of light to mark out where he had to go. Stewart rubbed his face free of the dust. He could see the clouds moving above him.

Moving fast.

Too fast, he thought.

Where he and his horse were standing was safe whilst the gloom of a million shadows covered them both from spying eyes, but what would happen when the clouds drifted away? When starlight cast its eerie illumination upon the top of the canyon rise and on the figures scrambling to clear its peak.

What then?

Would the stars betray them to the men who were still coming up the trail below him?

All they had to do was get over that rise, Stewart kept telling himself. No bullets could hit them once they cleared the ridge and started to make their descent into the canyon beyond, if there was a canyon beyond. The cowboy's heart started to pound as he dragged the weary horse ever upward towards the top of the world. What if there was nothing but a cliff there, he thought? What if the end of the trail was actually the end of the trail and there was nothing beyond but a deadly drop into oblivion? The thought was too much to be allowed to stick. There had to be a way down the other side into another maze of rock and dust, he told himself. There just had to be.

Stewart glanced over his shoulder. The torch still flickered like a beacon below him. Its light cast a warning. A warning of impending doom. The sound of the explosions returned to Stewart's memory. Then the echoing sound of the short but sickening battle which he had heard filled his thoughts once more. Whoever those gun-toting men were, bathed in the crimson glow of the flaming torch, they sure weren't no preachers.

The knees of his pants were ripped to his grazed and bloodied flesh as he continuously tripped and then staggered on. He was falling more than walking as his boots began to lose grip of the steepening incline, but he would not quit his attempt to find a way out of this satanic nightmare in which he had found himself innocently trapped.

'Gotta get to that rise.' He spat and tugged at his reins. 'Ya better quicken that pace, boy. If them critters see us we'll be eating carbine bullets. C'mon.'

The clouds were thinning. Gaps were appearing every few heartbeats. Gaps which allowed starlight to trace across the jagged peaks. The cowboy kept looking at the stars which appeared and then vanished as the black, brooding clouds moved faster and faster across the heavens.

'C'mon, horse.' He heard his voice virtually begging the mount to move faster. 'Them clouds ain't gonna be there long. When they've up and gone we're sitting ducks.'

He had to get over the top of the rise. All the cowboy had to do was reach the rise. Just reach the rise. It sounded a lot easier inside his head than it felt inside his blood-filled boots.

'C'mon, boy. Only another couple of hundred feet and we're safe.' The cowboy jerked at the reins and the horse reluctantly followed its master up towards their goal. 'Good boy. That's the way. We can make it easy as long as them clouds don't clear too damn quick.'

It was fear which gave the dog-tired cowboy the strength to continue staggering upwards. It was blind loyalty that enabled his horse to follow.

★   ★   ★

The torchlight flashed across the riders who flanked the wagon as its team of sure-footed mules laboured up the slope. Each grim-faced outlaw watched the unarmed horseman who had told them that this precarious route would lead them to where their fortune awaited. So far Jardine Barton had managed to fool his fellow outlaws into believing that he was at last taking them to what he had imaginatively named Whispering Skull. A place which Barton had invented years earlier.

The man who had once reigned supreme as their leader was now reduced to desperately trying to buy time. Time to figure a way out of the predicament he had found himself in. Time to come up with a way of besting Sharky before the hardened outlaw lost patience and simply killed him.

'Is ya sure this is the way, Jardine?' Rance Lee piped up as he aimed his horse after the lead horsemen. 'Seems like a mighty high rise to me. Ain't the kinda trail I figured would take us to Whispering Skull.'

Barton gave a brief glance at the horseman bathed in the light of the flickering torch, which was secured to the front rim of the wagon above Pecos Bill's head as he drove the wagon up the rugged trail.

'That's why nobody but me ever

found it, Rance,' Barton lied, with a wave of his free hand. 'If it was easy to get there then everybody would have found it.'

A few of the outlaws nodded. Sharky just looked across at Barton. He remained silent.

Higher and higher they rode. None of them was aware that there was a man less than a quarter-mile ahead of them desperately trying to reach the top of the trail. The clouds were still moving quickly. Gentle beams of eerie starlight traced across the trail before them like unquiet ghosts. The team of mules responded to the bullwhip in Pecos Bill's left hand and continued to haul the hefty vehicle over the rugged ground towards the very sky itself. The trail had been wide at the foot of the steep incline but as they gradually reached the spot from where Jeff Stewart had observed them, it started to narrow.

The black shadows of the massive rocks mingled with the rest of the dark terrain as Sharky Cole at last reined in and stopped the progress of his small but determined band of followers. Just behind the tail of Sharky's mount Elam, Lee and Harper sat astride their horses silently whilst on the other side of the wagon Tyler sat atop his white gelding, directly behind Jardine Barton.

Tyler had his hand resting upon his holstered gun. He, like the rest of the gang, was ready to kill Barton if he tried anything.

The unarmed Barton had tried to think of a plan for getting out of the situation he had created for himself over the years. Yet no matter how hard he tried Barton could not come up with anything that he thought might save his bacon.

No matter how hard he concentrated, his usually fertile mind could not think of a plan which might allow him to escape from the men who had once blindly done his bidding.

'Why'd we stop?' Barton asked.

Sharky eased himself off his saddle

and was grateful when his boots found the ground. He tied his reins to the lead mule's bridle and then walked around to where Barton sat.

'Reckon the animals need water.' Sharky spat the words at the mounted Barton.

Barton gave a slow nod. 'Ya right.'

'Listen up, Jardine. Are ya sure this is the way to Whispering Skull?' Sharky drew a cigar from his jacket and placed it between his teeth. 'Are ya truly sure? This sure don't look like it leads to no fortune to me. Looks like it leads up to heaven though.'

Barton chuckled. 'Don't go fretting about any of us ending up there, Sharky. I got me a feeling none of us will ever be welcome in heaven.'

Tey Tyler raised himself in his stirrups and looked down into the canyon. Even the shadows could not hide the fact that they were higher than any of them had ever been before. 'We sure are real high up, boys. I plumb don't like it. One false move and there ain't no way we could live if'n we fell into that hole.'

'Ain't that the truth,' Sharky agreed and grinned. 'Best we all try to keep away from the edge.'

Anxiously Barton watched the large gunman move closer to his mount but remained silent. He allowed the hand of the outlaw to rest upon his saddle before he cleared his throat.

'This is the way to Whispering Skull, Sharky,' Barton bluffed. 'Bin a long time since I was last here but I remember this trail.'

Sharky raised an eyebrow. 'I sure hope ya telling the truth, Jardine. I'd hate to have to waste all this time looking for something that don't even exist. I'd also hate to have to waste lead blowing ya head off ya shoulders.'

'Don't shoot too soon,' Barton said. 'We still got us a long way to go.'

'I hope ya telling the truth, Jardine,' Sharky warned as the rest of the men dismounted around the stationary wagon. 'Seems to me that this don't look like it leads no place. No place at all but I'll cut ya some slack. If'n ya hangs yaself with it, that ain't no skin off my rump.'

The words chilled Barton even more than the cold air which washed over them. 'We'll get there. Then ya will all be rich.'

'When?' Sharky asked.

'I ain't too sure.'

'Tomorrow?'

Barton swallowed hard. 'Could be. Depends.'

Sharky patted Barton's leg. 'Just heed my words. Ya know there ain't nothing I like more than killing folks, Jardine.'

'Sweet and fast?' Barton drawled.

Sharky nodded. 'Yep. Sweet and fast.'

'I don't want to end up another notch on ya grip,' Barton said fearlessly. 'I'll find Whispering Skull for ya. Ya can bet ya life on that.'

Sharky leaned closer to the horse and looked upward into Barton's torchlit features. Sharky had risked all of their lives to free their former leader from certain hanging, but he was doubtful that he or any of them would ever see the promised fortune.

'Are ya telling us the truth for once, Jardine boy?'

'Yep.' Barton nodded firmly.

'Ya sure?'

'Damn sure, Sharky.' Barton raised his voice, making the outlaw grab and squeeze his thigh with a powerful hand to demonstrate who was now the strongest member of the notorious gang.

'Ya don't ever shout at me again, Jardine. Ya hear?' Sharky growled. He released his grip and waved a fist at the horseman. 'For years I let ya rule the roost but that all ended when ya got yaself caught by the law.'

'Damn it all. Ya know I'm plumb crippled from being hunched up in that tiny cell for months, Sharky. I ain't got no muscle left for ya to wrestle with,' Barton complained.

Sharky Cole said nothing for a while. He just kept staring with bloodthirsty eyes up into the face of the man he still could not fathom.

'Do ya understand?' Sharky snarled.

'Yep.' Barton shrugged. 'You are the new boss. OK?'

Sharky grinned and stared upward for a few fleeting seconds; then he returned his burning eyes to Barton. 'What ya gonna do with your share of the treasure at Whispering Skull?'

'Reckon it might be a good time to retire,' Barton answered with a sigh.

'Yeah,' Sharky agreed. 'Me? I'm going to 'Frisco and buy a whorehouse and just wallow in the goods.'

Barton swallowed hard. He still did not know how he was ever going to escape from what was certain to be the brutal retribution of his former gang members once they discovered that there was no treasure waiting for them in the land of the dead. He rubbed his leg thoughtfully and stared all around them. Nothing but black shadows to be seen in every direction. Not even a hint of a means to escape from the expert gunmen who surrounded him.

Barton decided to change the subject. 'Tell me. Why'd we stop, Sharky?'

Sharky eased away from the horse and pulled the reins free of Barton's hands. He tied them to the bridle of the lead mule and then found a match. He struck it, cupped its flame around the end of his cigar and started to suck. He allowed the smoke to fill his lungs before he tossed the match over the edge of the high trail. His cruel eyes followed it down into the abyss before they returned to Barton.

'The animals need water and grain, Jardine,' Sharky said through a cloud of smoke. 'While the nags drink and eat, the boys can fill their bellies on jerky and stale bread. The bread's a tad wormy but we've had worse.'

'I'm used to eating worms,' Barton remarked. 'Seems like that's all them cooks dished out back at the prison. They ate like royalty but we just had the rotten leftovers. Whatever the rats left they gave us.'

'My heart bleeds for ya,' Sharky said with a laugh.

'I got me a feeling that when we reaches Whispering Skull I'm gonna end up dead,' Barton went on. 'Am I right?'

'That depends on you, Jardine.' Sharky stroked the head of Barton's horse. 'If we find out ya bin lying to us then I'll gut ya like a fish. Don't reckon ya ever seen anyone gutted. I sure have, a whole heap of times. Folks with their innards cut out don't die fast. They kinda linger. Savvy?'

Barton felt his stomach churn as though it understood the threat Sharky had just thrown at him. He dismounted and inhaled deeply in an effort to restrain his nerves from shattering.

'I sure don't cotton to them words, Sharky.'

'Heed them, Jardine,' Sharky said. 'Heed them and ya just might be alive when all this is over.'

Barton nodded and looked up at the outlaw seated on the wagon-driver's board. 'Can I have me some of that jerky Sharky mentioned, Bill?'

'Sure enough.' Pecos Bill clambered down and glanced at both men in turn before walking back towards the tail-gate. 'Got me a whole box full of jerky and bread back here.'

Barton felt the hand on his shoulder.

'Heed my words, Jardine,' Sharky warned again.

Suddenly Elroy Elam rushed to the shoulder of Barton's mount, raised a hand and pointed feverishly up the steep incline as the clouds drifted away.

'Look. Do ya see him?' Elam yelled excitedly.

Each of the outlaws looked up to where Elam was so frantically jabbing the air with his trigger finger. Eerie starlight lit up the summit of the jagged peaks ahead of them. A grey outline could be seen, traced across the highest point of the steep mountain where the rocks ended and the sky began.

For the first time Jeff Stewart and his

horse were visible to the deadly eyes of the outlaws as he desperately scrambled over the last few yards of rugged trail in an attempt to find sanctuary on the far side of the rocks.

'A man.' Elam spat. 'And he's leading a horse.'

'A dead man,' Sharky snarled as he drew both his guns and pulled back on their hammers until they locked. 'Whoever he is he's gonna meet his maker darn soon.'

They all watched as Sharky took aim with his .45s.

The exhausted cowboy was scrambling up towards the top of the trail but his equally tired horse was slowing his pace.

'Bet ya can't hit either of 'em,' Barton taunted. He took a bite of jerky and started to chew. 'He's out of range.'

'Oh yeah?' Sharky took two steps forward and then pulled his triggers towards the bellies of his guns. Both weapons spewed out blinding flame as their bullets raced from the barrels of the guns towards their targets.

As Barton had predicted both shots fell short.

Sharky forced his guns into their holsters and grabbed a rifle out of Harper's hands. With merciless expertise he cocked, aimed and fired the Winchester.

A scream of agony filled the night air as the figure arched in the starlight. He then buckled and disappeared over the very top of the high rim, taking his horse with him.

Sharky gave a satisfied grunt and threw the weapon back into Harper's hands. He turned and grinned at the men who were watching in awe.

'That's how ya kill fast and sweet, boys.'

Only Barton looked unimpressed as he continued to chew on his jerky. 'Not a bad shot, but I've seen better.'

'I got him, didn't I?' Sharky grinned and made his way back to Barton. Both men stood toe to toe and glared at one another.

'I wonder who he was?' Barton said with a smile.

'That don't matter none.' Sharky pushed past Barton and grabbed a chunk of dried meat from the box on the tailgate.

'It might,' Barton heard himself say. 'There are stories of ghosts in these mountains. Folks that just can't be killed coz they're already dead. Maybe that was one of them.'

The outlaws started to gather around their old leader.

Sharky sucked on his cigar. His eyes narrowed. 'Ya starting to spit out them tall tales again, Jardine?'

Barton made no reply.

'I know ya game.' Sharky tossed the cigar away. 'That was just some poor locobean who was running scared. I killed him and that's it. There ain't no such animal as ghosts or the like.'

Barton kept chewing and smiling.

'How'd we know ya killed him?'

Sharky inhaled. His chest expanded. 'I killed him OK,' Sharky insisted.

'I heard him scream.' Tyler nodded.

'Yep. I heard him grunt when that bullet hit him, Sharky,' Harper added.

Barton bit off another chunk of jerky. 'It don't matter none if'n he's dead or not, boys. The question is: who in tarnation is he and what's he doing here?'

The men all fell silent.

Sharky pushed his way to the tailgate, grabbed Barton's collar and pulled the man towards him. 'Stop trying to confuse the boys, Jardine. Anyone could see that it was just a stray cowpoke I shot.'

'A cowboy in these parts?' Barton felt the grip loosen as his words found their mark. 'I sure ain't seen me no steers anywhere close to here, Sharky. Think about it hard. Whoever that critter ya shot was, he sure couldn't be no cowpuncher.'

Sharky Cole rubbed his jaw. 'What ya playing at, Jardine?'

'Nothing,' Barton answered. 'C'mon.

I'll take ya to Whispering Skull right now.'

The grinning outlaws grabbed their reins and threw themselves back on to their saddles. All of them except one.

Confused, Sharky Cole glared at Barton.

He knew the cunning man was up to something, but what?

'Ya coming, Sharky?' Barton asked.

Sharky marched to his horse. 'Yep.'

9

It had felt like a red-hot branding-iron being thrust into his side as the bullet caught the slender Jeff Stewart. It had torn through his jacket and shirt before it bounced off his ribs. He had never been shot before and it hurt. Hurt real bad. The cowboy had just reached the very top of the canyon trail when the light of the stars had suddenly revealed his position to the deadly outlaws. As he had feared, the starlight betrayed him.

The rifle bullet which blasted from the barrel of Sharky Cole's Winchester only seconds earlier hit him before Stewart even heard the weapon being fired. The impact was like the kick of a bronco; it lifted the cowboy off his feet and propelled him helplessly through the night air. With the reins wrapped around his hands Stewart's weight had dragged the pitiful horse with him over the edge of the trail.

Both horse and master rolled across the harsh gravel until they hit the very lip of the canyon. The slope kept them moving faster than the cowboy could have ever thought possible. He had been thrown from the backs of mustangs but that had been nothing like this. He crashed and bounced ever downwards over the rugged rocks until he felt himself flying through the cold night air. Even stunned, he realized that he was no longer on solid ground. Now he was falling down into the unknown depths of a place hidden in shadow. Then he hit the cliff side and bounced until he collided with another jagged wall of solid rock. He was cartwheeling ever downwards. He brushed the rocks with every part of his flailing limbs and torso.

Stewart tried to see but even the light of a myriad stars could not penetrate the void into which both the cowboy and his mount were falling. The horse had made a sickening noise as it bounced the first time but then it stayed silent as its bones shattered on the unseen rocks it was crashing into on its long unstoppable descent.

His prized horse was dead, the dazed cowboy thought. Soon he too would be dead. He tried to cover his head with his arms but it was impossible.

The cowboy tried to see where he was heading but there was nothing but blackness wherever he looked. A blackness more fearsome than the men whom he had been trying to avoid for most of the long day and even longer night.

There was no way he could stop himself falling into the jaws of the dark abyss. He reached out with desperate fingers but he could find nothing to grasp but air. Over and over he rolled. Rocks caught almost every part of him as Stewart felt his entire body turning into a battered pulp.

The taste of blood filled his mouth but there was no time to spit. No time to do anything but keep falling.

The pain was now so intense that he could no longer feel the deep graze in his side where the rifle bullet had shattered a rib and torn a chunk of his flesh off his thin frame. Now every part of his body hurt with equal intensity.

He tried to see but the world was spinning like a top. All he knew for sure was that the black was gone. Now there was nothing but red. A cloud of red which covered his face as blood spewed from every cut on his head and body.

Then he hit something.

Something which was harder than he was. Something which stopped him from continuing his journey towards death.

Every particle of air was kicked out of his body by the sudden impact of his abrupt and unexpected halt.

It was a small ledge created a million years before time itself had even begun. It jutted out from the otherwise sheer cliff like a small shelf. It was barely big enough to allow an eagle to perch on it but had been big enough to stop the cowboy from continuing on down to his own demise.

The cowboy was on his face, clawing at the flat surface of the ledge as he tried to open his eyes. He could taste his own blood as streams of gore ran from his scarred head to his battered features. Features buried in the few inches of sandy dust that covered the flat rock.

The dazed Stewart lay flat on his belly for what seemed a lifetime as he tried to gather his wits. He suddenly realized that he had stopped falling. He heard the sickening sound coming from far below his resting place as the horse's body suddenly reached the bottom of the pit.

He was alive, he thought. Somehow, against all the odds, he was still alive, but in what condition? What if every bone in his young body was broken? What if he were trapped here and unable to move a muscle? Suddenly the idea of a quick death did not seem so bad to the stunned cowboy. It was sure a whole lot better than being helpless and prey to the eagles and vultures who would tear at his flesh until death eventually came.

He tilted his head and rubbed at his broken face until his eyes managed to see through the blurred ghosts which tormented him. Even dazed he realized he was on a ledge. A flat ledge which had somehow managed to bring him to a painful halt.

Stewart tried to rise but there was no wind left in him. It had all been kicked out of his body by the sudden impact as he landed on an immovable object.

'Where am I?' the cowboy whispered to himself.

Somehow he managed to raise his head and look to both sides, but his vision was hampered by the darkness and the ghostly war drums that kept pounding inside his battered skull.

Tentatively he eased his arms and legs apart to try and gauge the size of the rock shelf he was lying on. His left boot found the cliff wall whilst the right one found the edge of the small ledge.

It was no more than three feet wide but it had been big enough to stop him from following his dead mount down into the mysterious gorge.

He began to shake. Shake with muscle spasms of shock as the gravity of the situation started to dawn upon his still stunned mind. It was a miracle that he had not missed this tiny projection of rock, he thought. He ought to be as dead as his horse obviously was.

The cowboy closed his eyes and tried to calm himself so as to work out whether any part of his body was broken beyond repair. To his surprise nothing seemed to be broken apart from his nose and cheekbones. Determined to muster enough strength to rise off his belly, Stewart lay quite motionless for minutes, trying to regain his scrambled thoughts and work out what had happened to him. Slowly his mind began to reassemble its reason

and the cowboy felt his senses returning.

Then he recalled the bullet which
had knocked him off his feet and sent
him hurtling into the depths of some
unknown place. Pain started to torment
him again. The pain of a thousand cuts
and grazes. Yet Stewart was thankful for
every one of them. Pain told the
cowpuncher that he was still alive. Hurt
but still somehow alive. A whirlpool of
haze had filled his mind as he crashed
down the side of the canyon wall like a
rag doll. Now it was slowly lifting and
his thoughts became clearer.

Stewart pushed his gloved left hand,
into the dust and forced himself on to
his side. He was looking straight at the
rocks. A few sparkles of frosty moisture
danced in the dim light of the stars,
telling him what he was staring at.

He looked up. It was a strange sight.

A star-filled sky, set above the
blackest of rocks.

He could actually see the very spot
from where he had fallen. Then, to his

horror, he saw the shimmering glow of the crimson light as it rippled against the rocks. Stewart remained quite still as the sound of the wagon's chains and horses' hoofs drifted down to where he lay helpless.

The torchlight grew brighter, looking like a monstrous firefly above the wagon on which the torch stood. Stewart screwed up his eyes as blood trailed down his face from his torn scalp. He could see the riders atop their mounts bathed in the scarlet hue of the torchlight. He could hear the muffled sounds of them talking to one another. He could also see the metal barrels of their Winchesters as the red light of the torch danced along them.

The men had come to finish the job, he reasoned.

10

The flames of the torch tied to the wagon flickered against the night sky as Pecos Bill hauled back on the hefty reins and brought his mule team to a halt. In front of him the six horsemen were standing at the highest point of the canyon rise, staring down into the black abyss. They had made good time reaching the place where they had all seen Sharky Cole's bullet hit the unknown man who had been leading his horse close to the top of one of the mountain range's highest points. They could still see the marks on the ground where the cowboy had been lifted off his feet and sent flying backwards towards the perilous edge of the cliff, dragging his mount with him.

The way the ground dipped and sloped as the natural trail went round the corner of the wall of rock raised doubts in the outlaws' minds as to the cowboy's fate. There was a blind spot at the trail's highest point. A drop of more than twenty feet separated the two points. Each of the riders knew that a man and horse could have fallen here and appeared to have gone over the edge, but could still have been able to get back on their feet without anyone actually seeing them.

One by one the outlaws drew rein. Sharky Cole was first to drop from his high saddle and reach the blood-splattered rocks which showed signs that both man and beast had actually fallen through the black depths to the canyon floor far below.

He knelt, leaned over the edge and looked down into the darkness. For a few moments Sharky brooded. Then he turned to Harper, who was still mounted.

'Bring that torch to me, Bo,' he ordered. 'I want to check something.'

Bo Harper stood in his stirrups, stretched across from his horse and plucked the torch from the wagon behind Pecos Bill's back. The outlaw tapped his spurs and heeled his mount to walk to where Sharky was kneeling.

'Here ya go, Sharky,' Harper said, tossing the blazing torch down. 'What ya seen?'

'I ain't seen nothing,' Sharky growled. 'That's why I needs me the torch.'

The other outlaws moved closer to where Sharky knelt.

'That's sure an awful long way down,' Elam observed. He returned to his horse and mounted up again. 'I sure don't wanna fall down there.'

Rance Lee exhaled loudly and shook his head. 'Ain't no way a man could live if he fell over that rim, boys. That critter Sharky shot gotta be dead.'

The others all snorted in agreement. All but Jardine Barton, who remained silent as he watched Sharky with a narrowed, cunning gaze.

Screwing up his eyes Sharky fanned the torch over the sheer drop. The fiery end of the torch hissed and spat in the chill breeze that came up from the depths into which Sharky was staring. Glowing red embers floated all around the outlaws.

'Can ya see him, Sharky?' Barton asked. He rested a hand on his saddle horn and kept watching the deadly outlaw. 'Can ya, Sharky? Can ya see the varmint ya reckon ya shot? Is he down there?'

There was a long silence before Sharky straightened up and walked back to the wagon with the torch in his grip. He handed the long staff of light back to the wagon driver and gave a shrug. He glared at Barton.

'Nope. I couldn't see nothing down there but a whole mess of black.' Sharky pulled out a fresh cigar, rammed it between his dark teeth, bit off its end and spat. 'But I'll tell ya something, Jardine.'

'What would that be?' Barton enquired.

'He sure must be dead.' Sharky ran a

match along his pants leg and raised its flame to his cigar tip. 'Real dead.'

'Reckon so.' Barton nodded. 'Anyone dropping into that hole gotta be dead. If'n he did fall over that rock lip, that is.'

Sharky tossed the match away and stepped even closer to Barton. He blew a line of smoke up at the horseman. 'Ya reckon he didn't fall over there, Jardine?'

Barton shrugged. 'He might have rolled down this trail and then got back on his nag and spurred. The trail goes all the way down to the next canyon's mouth. He might be a mile or so down yonder by now for all we know.'

'Ya wrong.' Sharky grinned.

'Ya sure?'

'Yep. I'm damn sure, Jardine.'

'OK. I'll admit the edge of them rocks looks a tad beaten up as if someone skidded on the ground but — '

Barton had not had time to finish his sentence when he saw the palms of

Sharky's gloves being waved under his nose. Gloves covered in blood. Blood the outlaw had found on the rocks he had been investigating so carefully.

'See this, Jardine. Nice and fresh blood. This is the blood of the critter I shot. It's all over them rocks,' Sharky announced proudly. 'It goes across the ground and over them rocks and beyond. That's why I wanted the torch to see what was so sticky. Yep. That varmint is dead. My bullet sent him and his nag clean over that trail edge just like I said. They didn't spur down yonder. They're up and dead OK. Man and nag went flying out into the canyon and that sure ain't a healthy thing to do.'

Barton raised his eyebrows. 'I'd say ya was right. They went flying OK, Sharky. Ya still the best shot I ever seen.'

'And don't forget it.' Sharky drew deeply on his cigar, then gave out a grunt. He strode to his mount, grabbed his reins, stepped into a stirrup and mounted. He dragged his horse hard to his left, then jabbed his spurs into its flesh. The horse began to trot down the steep sloping trail towards the next canyon.

'C'mon, boys. We got us some treasure to find,' Sharky bellowed out. 'C'mon, Jardine. I'd hate for ya to lag behind me and start eating my dust.'

Barton turned his horse and followed as the rest of the riders and the wagon trailed Sharky down into the depths of even darker shadows.

Lee eased his horse next to Barton's as they made their way down the slope.

'How long do ya figure before we gets to Whispering Skull, Jardine?' Lee asked.

Barton tilted his head as the beginnings of a plan started to take root in his mind. 'Not too long, Rance. Hardly no time at all.'

11

Captain Jerome Hyde brushed down his dusty tunic with his white gauntlets and gave his timepiece a quick glance. He sighed at the faint photographic image of his long-dead sister captured within its lid. It was the only likeness she had ever had taken before Barton had slain her. The officer sighed deeply, then snapped the golden lid shut, gathered up the chain and slid the watch back into his breast pocket.

'It will not be long now, dearest Laura,' Hyde whispered to himself. 'Soon I shall make him pay for what he did to you, little sister.'

Hyde tilted his head and looked at the half-dozen cavalrymen who had been chosen by Sergeant Riley to accompany them through the devilish mountain canyons in pursuit of the gang of villainous killers who had destroyed practically the entire prison.

The soldiers were raw but Riley considered them the pick of the bunch and Hyde had learned that it did not pay to disagree with the experienced sergeant. If Riley said they were the best then they were. Fiery torches lit up the courtyard as the majority of his men went about their duties.

Captain Hyde raised a hand and walked around the freshly watered and grained horses as the last of their saddles were being secured. Hyde noted that Riley had cut six of the mules out from the last of the supply wagons' traces and ensured they were laden down with a voluminous supply of both fresh water and provisions.

As the officer reached the centre of the yard where his men had attempted to bury all of the bodies they had found slaughtered within what remained of Fort Addams he saw Riley move towards him. It was like watching the approach of a bear. Riley had muscles such as most men never imagined possible and it was said that if angered he knew how to use every one of them.

'Everything seems to be in order, Sergeant,' Hyde said, nodding.

'The men I picked are ready, Captain,' Riley boomed out.

'Good.' Hyde gestured with one of his gauntlets.

'Does ya think it's wise for us to head out before sunrise, sir?' Riley leaned over and rested his knuckles on his black-belted hips. 'Them trails are real dangerous.'

Hyde raised an eyebrow. 'I thought you knew them like the back of your hand, Sergeant? Isn't that what you've been telling me since I was sent out here to this God-forsaken land?'

'That's perfectly right, Captain,' Riley nodded. 'But I ain't never liked riding through them canyons after dark. They gets mighty black shadows out there and ya can't see the ears of ya horse, let alone anything else.'

'We shall have torches,' Hyde said. 'Two men will carry them, riding slightly ahead of the rest of us so we can follow the outlaws' hoof tracks. Isn't that what you said?'

Riley grinned shyly. 'Indeed. Yep, I said that. I just never hanker for going into the land of the dead even when I can see everything that's around me. Them canyons get blacker than anything and it can be a little dangerous.'

'How?'

'Ya gotta watch out for holes in the ground, Captain,' Riley gestured. 'Big deep holes that can break ya horse's legs if'n it goes into one.'

'Holes?' Hyde was curious. 'You mean rabbit holes?'

Riley shook his head. 'Nope. It was men and women that made them holes out there. The Shoshoni lived in holes until they left this land. That's how they survived the seasons. They'd dig a deep hole and live in it all year round. It was cooler in the summer and just a tad above freezing in the winter. Them Injuns might have up and gone but them holes are still out there. Thousands of them.'

Hyde sighed. 'No problem. We shall not allow our mounts to go faster than walking pace until sunrise.' Hyde turned to the six troopers who were waiting close to the horses and mules.

Riley gave a nod. 'Genius thinking, Captain.'

Hyde walked to the mounts and the soldiers. 'I thank you, men. This is going to be a very dangerous mission that we are about to undertake but I have full confidence in all of you. Sergeant Riley has said that you are the best of our new recruits and his word is fine with me. Mount.'

The men started to mount as Hyde reached his own horse and pulled its reins free of the makeshift tethering line. He held on to his horse's mane and stepped into his stirrup. In one fluid action the officer was astride his horse.

Sergeant Riley handed large torch poles to two of the mounted troopers and ran a match along his pants leg to ignite their well-oiled rags. He then ran to his own horse and threw his hefty body up on to his saddle.

'Ready, sir.' Riley saluted.

Captain Hyde turned his horse and tapped his spurs until the animal was facing what remained of the once solid gates. He waved his arm.

'Forward ho.'

Slowly, with the two torch-bearing troopers at the head of the small caravan the cavalrymen started out towards the place Riley always referred to as the land of the dead.

★　★　★

Along with a thousand war drums pounding inside the cowpuncher's head, the stars that had earlier betrayed him had suddenly been obscured by the approach of ominous, fast-moving storm clouds. The entire mountain range became blanketed by them as they angrily swirled like heavenly whirlpools. Off in the distance, white flashes of lightning splintered across them as they rapidly made their way to where the cowboy was trapped.

After what felt like a lifetime, Stewart had at last managed to get his aching body into a sitting position upon the small ledge. It had taken him so long to achieve this task that the blood which covered his body had dried and the cuts scabbed over. But, for all the evidence that there was indeed a storm on its way, Stewart could not hear the thunderclaps from his precarious perch.

The boots on his long outstretched legs were dangling just over the lip of the ledge. The injured cowboy leaned his back against the wall of rough rock and stared out across the expanse of shadows before him. There had been nothing to see since the wagon had continued on its way, taking its flaming torch with it. Stewart had never prayed so devoutly before the moment he had seen the outlaw leaning over the top of the ridge waving the fiery torch.

When his blurred eyes had spotted Sharky Cole far above him the cowboy had done what most men do when faced with something they cannot control. He had started to beg his maker not to allow any of the gunmen to see him lying helplessly on the narrow ledge.

It had worked. They had not seen him.

Their bullets had not rained down upon him, as he had dreaded, and he was still alive. Bruised and battered but still alive.

Stewart was sucking in air hard and fast as he vainly tried to find the strength to stand. It was no good. His legs were still as weak as those of a baby. Every inch of his lean frame was contused or cut. Reluctantly, even in his dazed state of mind, he knew that it was far safer if he waited until sunup before even attempting to get to his feet.

Stewart ran a gloved hand across the surface of the rock he sat upon. It was slippery with the night frost.

'I gotta get me some shut-eye,' the cowboy said aloud as he flexed his fingers. Even the slightest movement sent lightning bolts of pain through him. 'Close ya eyes, Jeff. Sleep. Ya can't go no place until ya can see the lie of the land.'

The words made sense even when uttered by a man who had been knocked almost unconscious on his way down to this narrow ledge, but no matter how much sense they made Stewart was determined to stay awake.

He knew that although sleep might be restful it might also prove fatal. What happened if he rolled off this tiny perch and fell into the canyon? The unspoken question haunted and frightened the cowboy.

Stewart had seen his horse pass him in mid air. It had continued to fall for what had seemed an awfully long time before he had heard the sickening sound of it hitting the floor of the canyon. To Stewart that meant that the ledge which had saved his life was still far too high to roll off in your sleep without fatal consequences.

He had to wait until sunrise.

There was no other way.

Even hampered by the blackness that showed no signs of relenting the cowboy began to check himself over with his hands to try once again to see if he was in one piece. He knew what broken bones felt like. As a cowboy he had encountered a lot of them over the years. Some broken bones were just a nuisance whilst others could be fatal.

He managed to reach his boots. Both spurs had been ripped from his boots on the way down the cliff face. Stewart did not care, as to use spurs you needed a horse and that luxury had been stolen from him.

His fingers moved up his pants legs. Both were torn up to the knees. He could feel his exposed flesh. Flesh which seemed far rougher than normal. Although Stewart could not see them he knew that both his legs had been cut up pretty badly.

Everything seemed to be fine until his hands reached his ribs and found the hideous bullet wound. He gritted his teeth and gave out a painful howl of pain when he came across the chunk of missing flesh and felt the broken rib protruding out of his side.

'Damn it all,' he spat as he realized the course of the bullet that had torn through his jacket and shirt and carved a path across his ribcage. 'That bastard took a mighty big lump out of me by the feel of it. Damn.'

There was no way of knowing what the time was or when the sun would rise again and start to burn its victims alive, as was its daily ritual. All Stewart could do was sit and wait. Wait to find out how bad his situation actually was.

A score of thoughts raced through the cowboy's head.

Each one no better than the other.

Which way should he go after dawn? Up or down? Once the sun rose he could not remain where he was unless he wanted to be burned alive by its merciless rays. Which would be easier: to attempt to climb back up the trail above him, or to venture down to where his horse had crashed into the canyon floor?

There was no way of telling until sun-up.

He rubbed his throat. He was thirsty. He recalled the full canteens which had been hanging from his saddle horn. The choice of which way to go seemed to have been made for him. If he wanted to drink that precious liquid he had to try to find those canteens.

Another thought flashed into his mind.

What if it was impossible to go in either direction?

What if there was no way off this small ledge of solid rock?

A cold chill raced through his body.

It had nothing to do with the icy temperature, which was causing frost to cover him. It was the thought of being trapped up on a ledge unable to find a way of climbing away from the place that had saved his life.

If only he had his cutting rope, but that, like the canteens, was tied to his saddle horn. He took some deep breaths, as if trying to remain calm. With each passing moment it grew harder and harder to stop himself from simply crying out like a wounded coyote.

Stewart lowered his chin until it rested on his bandanna. A pain tore through his face. He raised both hands and felt his broken face. It hurt. Every inch of his face felt as if it had been mule-kicked. His nose was shattered and his chin did not seem to be where it should be. He removed his right glove and inspected his face more carefully with his fingertips.

His teeth were loose, but remained in his gums, yet his face was cut to ribbons. Both Stewart's eyes were swollen and tender to even the most tender of touches.

'No wonder I can't see straight,' the young man mumbled.

He put his glove on again and ran it across the cold rock beside him. He rubbed the gathered frost into his face and lips. It felt good for the briefest of moments.

Suddenly a strange noise filled the cowboy's ears. It echoed along the canyon, riding upon the cold breeze. The cowboy sat forward. It was a haunting sound, which Stewart was unable to identify.

Again and again he heard its chilling tune. It was as though the very air itself was performing an aria straight from the depths of the black shadows that were gathered around him on all sides.

The cowboy tried to move but he was still unable to venture anywhere amid the eerie shadows. He listened hard and felt his heart start to pound once again as his mind tried to work out what was making the frightening noise.

Was it just the wind?

The terrified youngster closed his eyes but the sound kept finding his battered soul. Was it some animal out there, calling to warn that it would soon be on the prowl?

Stewart rubbed his face.

The mysterious noise grew first louder and then fainter with every beat of his heart. Was that the sound of a living creature, he asked himself?

Or was it something else?

Something he had yet to encounter.

The only sound it seemed to resemble was one that he had heard only once before, far to the north when he had been trying to gather up stray mavericks. That had been the wail of a prowling cougar. Some Indians, he had heard, feared the sound as a harbinger of death.

The tormented cowboy took a deep breath and tried to find his tobacco pouch in his jacket pocket. His fingers were shaking as he pulled the pouch free and took a slim gummed paper out of the small bag.

As he rolled a cigarette Stewart began to realize that in truth this ghoulish noise was like nothing he had ever heard before. It was no cougar. No coyote or bear.

This was something new.

He ran his tongue across the gummed edge of the paper, and rolled the cigarette into shape. He put the narrow tube of paper in the corner of his bruised mouth.

He found a match and struck it across his belt buckle. The flame erupted and quickly he lit the cigarette before the breeze could blow the flame out. As he inhaled the smoke he prayed that it might help settle his broken nerves and enable him to think clearly again.

The sound suddenly grew louder.

A choir of ghosts were singing out there somewhere, he told himself. Singing for all they were worth.

Stewart swallowed hard. Even though he could see nothing, he could smell the tobacco smoke encircling his bruised and battered head before it travelled away from the high ledge.

'For Pete's sake, what in tarnation is

that?' he muttered through loose teeth and smoke. He sucked hard on the flimsy cigarette again, trying to find either courage or answers in the smouldering tobacco. 'Damn it all. This sure has bin one real bad day and I got me a feeling it'll get worse before it gets better.'

The unearthly choir continued.

12

The gang of deadly outlaws had managed to reach the canyon floor before the unholy sound rolled out of the darkness and washed over them. The high-walled canyon seemed to act like a tunnel for the strange noise that chilled the hearts and souls of those who heard it. Pecos Bill slammed his boot on to the long brake pole and forced his team of mules to halt as one by one the horsemen who surrounded the wagon dragged their mounts to an abrupt stop. The two riders at the head of the small group steadied their skittish horses. One of them seemed totally calm whilst the other was obviously unnerved.

For the first time since any of the other outlaws had known Sharky Cole they were witnessing a man who appeared to be genuinely fearful. The rugged features of Sharky were lit up in the flickering light of the torch and were drowning in a confused ocean of dread.

Barton watched the man who had replaced him as gang leader with more than a hint of concealed amusement. He remained silent as Sharky kept looking all around them as the heart-stopping sound filled the black air.

'What is that, Jardine?' Sharky snapped. He steadied his mount and drew close to Barton. 'Ya hear it? What's making that damn noise?'

The cunning Barton had no idea what was making the ghostly sounds which seemed to be flowing through the air from the heart of the canyon's twisting trails, but he had heard it before. A long time ago when he had outwitted not only a posse but the land of the dead itself. Whatever it was, Barton had never been one to miss an opportunity to gain the upper hand on the outlaw, who was obviously unnerved. Barton raised an eyebrow and stared at Sharky. Even in the dim torchlight he could see the terror in his face as Sharky nodded furiously.

'Tell me, Jardine,' Sharky growled, 'what in tarnation is that damn noise?'

'That's the ghosts that guard the Skull,' Barton said without even the glimmer of any emotion on his face. 'Didn't I mention that Whispering Skull is guarded by demons and ghosts?'

Sharky grabbed Barton's arm and almost hauled him from his saddle.

'What?' he raged frantically.

'Ya heard me,' Barton continued. 'It's the ghosts that guard the skull down yonder. I seen them with my own eyes the last time I was here. That's why I left empty-handed.'

Sharky felt his throat tighten. 'There ain't no such animal as ghosts. Ya joshing with me.'

Barton shrugged.

'Sure sounds like ghosts,' Elam said.

Lee nodded. 'Yep. A whole herd of the critters.'

'Almost sounds like folks singing, to

me,' Harper offered.

Sharky's eyes darted from face to face as he loosened his grip and released Barton. He rubbed his sweat-soaked face along his sleeve and gave a gruff half-hearted chuckle.

'Must be something else,' he insisted. He searched frantically for a cigar in his pockets. 'This damned place is full of loco things. Yep. It's gotta be something else.'

'But Jardine said he seen them,' Elam said.

'He must have bin loco with thirst.' Sharky nodded and kept searching his pockets. 'Folks see a lot of things when they ain't had enough water. Ain't that right, Jardine?'

'Ya could be right.' Barton smiled.

'Sure I'm right,' Sharky insisted.

Barton gathered up his reins, confidently tapped his spurs and edged his mount forward into the shadows.

'C'mon, Sharky. Ain't no call to be feared,' he said over his shoulder. 'After all, how can ghosts hurt us?'

Sharky knew that each of the men was watching his every move as he eventually found a long, twisted cigar and placed it between his teeth.

Again he forced a chuckle. 'Me scared? That's a joke. Ya all knows I ain't feared of nothing.'

The strange noise continued to thrum through the darkness and fill their even darker hearts with dread. They all shared the sense of trepidation but only Sharky seemed actually to be showing his uneasiness.

'I know what that is. It's a train someplace and the wind is carrying the sound. That's it. It's a damn train.'

'Ain't no trains or track for over two hundred miles from here, Sharky.' Harper laughed and pointed a finger at their new leader. 'Whatever it is making that hullabaloo it sure ain't no train.'

Anger started to fester like a barrel of fiery worms inside Sharky. He glared at Harper silently as the outlaw kept laughing at him.

Pecos Bill slapped the reins down on the backs of the mules and started the wagon rolling after Barton. The outlaw leaned over from his high seat and looked down at Sharky as the outlaw struck a match and lit his cigar. 'Are ya coming or not? Old Jardine is back on the trail, Sharky. Don't ya wanna get to Whispering Skull?'

The other riders tapped their spurs and followed the wagon as it was expertly driven along the uneven trail after the seemingly fearless Barton.

As Harper passed Sharky he patted the trembling man's back.

'C'mon, Sharky. Ain't nothing to be feared of. Jardine will make sure no monsters git ya.' He laughed and rode on.

His laughter tormented the outlaw's soul. A fury suddenly erupted like a volcano. Snarling like a madman Sharky drew one of his guns, cocked its hammer and fired once. The back of Harper's head shattered as the bullet drove through his skull.

The sound rocked the canyon. The other riders drew rein and swiftly turned just in time to see Bo Harper flying from his saddle and crashing into the ungiving ground. Sharky fanned his hammer over and over until every bullet had been sent into the dead outlaw's corpse.

Jardine Barton stopped his mount. Then, reassured that it was not he who had been shot, he slowly swung round and stared in the eerie crimson light of the torch at the horrific scene. A fountain of blood was spurting from the vengeful head wound that had ended the outlaw's existence. Barton let out a sigh of relief.

'What ya do that for?' Elam yelled at Sharky as the scowling outlaw replaced the spent casings in his gun with fresh bullets from his belt.

'Why? Bo made the mistake of trying to say I was feared,' Sharky snarled back. 'I'll kill the whole pack of ya if anyone else tries to make out I'm scared.'

The outlaws watched as Sharky stabbed his spurs into the flanks of his horse and rode to where Barton was waiting. He did not return the weapon to his holster but kept it cocked and ready.

'C'mon, ya bunch of old women,' Sharky called out, riding ahead of the small band of outlaws. 'Does ya want a written invitation?'

Barton rubbed the dust from his eyes as the rest of the men caught up with him. Then he too spurred his horse on. They were all making for the land of the dead. A land which had claimed one more victim.

As the riders continued on they heard the strange noise coming to them again out of the darkness. It seemed to be getting louder and louder the further along the trail they went.

'What is that noise really, Jardine?' Elam asked, coming to ride level with the man who had once been their leader.

Without turning his head Barton
replied.

'Only ghosts, Elroy.'

'Whose ghosts?'

'Ours.'

13

It was as though a mystical wizard had waved a wand at the black sky above the desolate place known as the land of the dead and had abruptly changed the entire landscape. At first an amber glow swept from the horizon up and over the distant mountain ranges, without touching any of the ancient rocky spires or canyons. Then the sun rose up above the distant pinnacles and sent beams of blinding light racing over everything below. With the light came the heat.

The monstrous heat.

The frost-covered rocks suddenly started to yield to the heat and mist rose heavenwards. The cowboy was temporarily blinded as the sun blazed straight at him. He covered his scarred features with his hands, then he felt the cold of the night being sucked from his every sinew.

Stewart gave out a huge sigh of relief. He was still alive.

He had survived.

As he lowered his hands once more another sensation filled his sleep-starved mind. It had not been a nightmare that had taunted him for hours, after all. It had all been true. All of the horrors he had experienced had been real.

He was indeed trapped on a perilous ledge.

The cowboy shook his head in an attempt to adjust his eyes to the bright morning light. For the first time he was able to see exactly where he was. Even in his darkest thoughts he had not imagined his plight to be quite as bad as this. The true magnitude of his situation dawned on the bruised cow-poke.

He drew a sharp breath. 'Hell. I'm in worse trouble than I figured.'

Cautiously he eased himself to the very edge of the small slab of rock and looked down. His eyes widened.

He was roughly thirty feet above the canyon floor. He darted his gaze all around him. The sides of the canyon were jagged. It was a vertical drop from where he sat to where he could see his dead horse. He looked up, but that only filled him with even more horror. As the sunlight hit the wall he could see the marks of dried blood across its surface. It was his blood and that of his broken mount. Every impact they had made on their fateful fall was marked in sickening red stains upon the craggy surface.

Stewart tried to stretch his limbs to see how much agility he had retained. The cowboy had hurt before, as was usual in his trade, but he had never hurt like he hurt now. Every muscle in his lean frame screamed at even the slightest of movements. He cast his attention down to his torn trail gear and the dark, dried blood which covered his skin. For the first time since he had arrived at this small chunk of rock he could actually see his injuries. No bronco-busting accident had ever left him looking this bad, he thought.

Like a nervous mountain cat he kept moving upon the tiny ledge in a vain attempt to find a safe way down. If there was one he sure could not find it.

Stewart rested and gazed down at the canteens still tied to the horn of his saddle below him. He rubbed his dry throat. He needed a damn drink, his mind kept telling him. A long, slow swallow of water.

Water to wash away the taste of blood from his mouth. The broken body of the dead mount was within roping distance, he thought. The trouble was that his damn cutting rope was tied right next to the canteens.

Down there.

The distance between them tormented him. Thirty feet might just as well have been a thousand miles. He was trapped. Trapped to wait and die.

The first thought that came to his mind was: could he dangle over the lip of the ledge and drop?

Sure he could. If he wanted to break both his legs.

The canyon floor was hard. It must be quite as hard as the rocks against which he was leaning, he thought. The way his horse was spread out in the pool of its own dried gore told the cowboy that the ground had no yield in it. Anything that landed there just broke.

Stewart went to remove his torn top coat when another idea came into his mind. He could make a rope out of his clothing if he tied it all together. But what would he secure it to? The ledge had defeated him again.

'Damn it all,' he raged. 'Think, boy. Think.'

There must be a way out of this mess. Stewart forced himself up on to his unsteady legs and gazed down to where he had watched the torch of the gunmen pass hours earlier. He rubbed his throat again and again whilst he looked down at the precious canteens. Canteens heavy with water.

Stewart was suddenly aware of something far above him. A huge shadow came suddenly between the cowboy and the sun. He looked up and saw the majestic span of a vulture's wings as it circled on the rising warm air.

The bird could smell the scent of death. Death upon which it craved to banquet down in the canyon.

The shadow fell upon the dead horse below him. Stewart knew that it was the way of things that one critter feasted upon the flesh of other critters in the wilderness. Then he became concerned. What if the sharp beaks of vultures not only tore the meat off his horse's bones but also ripped open the canteens? The water would be gone for ever. Soaked up by the dry ground and the growing heat of the sun.

A sudden urgency filled the cowboy's soul. What could he do? He had to get down there and salvage his water real fast. But how?

Then yet another thought came to

Stewart's mind.

The unearthly sound he had heard for hours during the darkest part of the night was gone. Now only the noise of the rocks warming up as the rays of the sun hit them filled the air.

Straining his eyes Stewart tried to see what lay far to the south in the direction the horsemen had taken with their wagon. It was impossible. The heat haze and the rising mist blurred everything more than a quarter of a mile from where he was standing.

Then suddenly he heard something familiar.

It was the sound of horses' hoofs echoing off the walls of the canyon. He turned and looked in the opposite direction.

He raised a hand to shield his eyes. Then he saw them.

Eight riders.

For a brief moment he thought the gunmen had gone in a complete circle and were now returning. Then Stewart knew these were no gunfighters he was looking at. His prayers had been answered.

He rubbed his face. Even the coating of white dust which covered their uniforms could not hide the truth from the cowboy.

'Well I'll be a toad-sucking varmint. Soldier boys,' Stewart muttered joyfully. 'A whole mess of them and they're headed to where my dead horse is.'

No sooner had the joyous words made their way through his loose teeth and scarred lips that Stewart saw the white gauntlet of the lead rider rise and point in his direction. They had spotted him, Stewart thought.

Dust rose up off the hoofs of the riders and their pack mules. The small troop of cavalrymen started to increase their pace towards him.

As dust rose up off the hoofs of the approaching riders a stiff breeze suddenly caught the cowboy and made him turn. He stared off in the direction where he had last seen the torchlight of the outlaws vanishing into the night gloom hours before.

Stewart steadied his weary frame against the rock-face. Then he heard the strange, haunting sound that had troubled him earlier. Whatever the noise was it seemed to ride on the wind like the bugle call of a phantom horseman.

The cowboy returned his attention to the small troop of soldiers again. A broken smile crossed his bloodstained features.

'Leastways I'm gonna be up and saved,' the cowboy said, and looked up at the blue sky. He winked, then sat down again. His legs dangled over the high precipice.

All he could do now was wait.

Wait to be rescued.

        ★   ★   ★

The haunting sound which had already reached the stranded cowboy a few miles behind the labouring wagon and its weary outriders seemed to torment Sharky Cole as he led them further into the unknown terrain. The brutal outlaw who had already demonstrated his unpredictability by slaying Bo Harper suddenly jerked his horse to an abrupt stop. He raised himself in his stirrups to listen once again to the eerie noise which had returned to torment them. His unstable mind wondered if the words spoken by Barton about it being a choir of ghosts beckoning them to their deaths were true. This was called the land of the dead, he silently reasoned. No matter how hard he tried Sharky could not work out what the noise actually was. Was it an animal he had never encountered before, or was it something else? Something more in keeping with the ancient tales of sirens he had heard of during his youth.

The stifling mist which continued to rise from the rocks as the sun crept through the canyon shrouded everything from view at ground level. The only things which were visible were the peaks of the strange mountain-top formations. The towering spires and lopsided layers of rock loomed like gigantic monsters ready to awaken and strike down on the mere mortals below their lofty heights.

Sharky was tired and even more dangerous than ever. He had waited years to become the leader of this gang, and nothing but death would strip him of that. He growled like a wounded animal as he fought his weariness.

'That damn noise is making my head burst,' he yelled out.

None of the others uttered a word. They simply watched the gun-wielding outlaw who had already killed one of their own and wondered whether they might be next to taste his venomous lead. Yet it was not the fear of Sharky that chilled them to the bone. It was the knowledge that they were trapped. Trapped within the ever-narrowing gulches and canyons. The rocks were crackling like bacon in a skillet all around them as the blazing rays of the sun sucked up the frost that covered their surfaces and turned it into a noisome fog that drifted through the canyon like spectres as the unearthly sound moved on a soundless breeze.

Unable to control the cocktail of fear and weariness Sharky raised his gun and fired into the whirlpool of cloud that surrounded them. Again and again he sent red-hot deafening tapers into the white mist. He did not stop until his .45 was empty.

'What's making that cursed noise, Jardine?' Sharky snarled. He shook the casings from his smoking chambers and forced fresh bullets back into his Colt. 'It's driving me loco.'

'Reckon it ain't ghosts, Sharky,' Barton said, trying to calm the terrified man before he did actually turn his weapons on the rest of them. 'Reckon it must be some kinda natural thing. Like wind being squeezed through a narrow tunnel or the like.'

The troubled Sharky glanced at Barton, who had stopped his own mount next to his. He had never seen Barton show any signs of anything but total assurance in all the days they had ridden together. Barton never got scared of anything or anyone.

'Ya reckon?' Sharky snapped his gun shut.

'Yep,' Barton replied.

Sharky nodded furiously. 'That's what I was reckoning.'

Barton said nothing more. For countless hours he had been trying to think of a way of getting the better of Sharky before he ended up like Harper. His fertile imagination had never been so active but still had not found an answer until now. Now he looked at the fog and he knew that was the key. All he had to do was bide his time and wait for the perfect opportunity to make his bid for freedom.

Sharky looked at Barton who remained emotionless. He could barely see the outlaw as the fog crept closer and closer around them.

'When we gonna get to Whispering Skull, Jardine?' Sharky asked, thrusting the gun barrel under Barton's chin.

'Don't go giving me no more eyewash like ya done before. This time I want the truth or I'll blow ya head clean off. When we gonna reach the treasure?'

Barton eased himself briefly off his saddle to let the breeze cool his underside. He then seated himself again and looped his reins around the saddle horn.

'To tell ya the truth I ain't got a damn clue, Sharky.'

Sharky's expression altered dramatically. 'Huh? I thought ya knew exactly where we was?'

Ignoring the cold steel that was pressed into his throat, Barton nodded, then looked over his shoulder at the others as they made their way through the mist towards them. The canyon floor was now totally irregular; it was impossible for the wagon to progress any further. It slanted so severely that even the usually sure-footed mules were having trouble negotiating its boulder-littered surface. Barton looked back at Sharky.

'I was pretty sure I knew where we was until this damn mist rose up after sunrise, Sharky,' Barton lied. 'But I ain't too sure we're in the right canyon any more. Maybe when it lifts I'll be able to get my bearings.'

'And the god-awful ruckus is just the wind?' Sharky pressed, rubbing his temple with his free hand. 'Is that right? Is it?'

'Yep.' Barton was still thinking. His gaze darted all around them as he searched for a way to escape. 'Nothing but a real sharp breeze cutting through something. Damned if I can figure what, though.'

Sharky, open-mouthed, lowered his gun. 'I got me a real bad feeling that this is the first time ya ever told me the truth, Jardine.'

'Maybe it is.'

'Then why does that trouble me so much?' Sharky looked ahead and then all around them as one by one the other outlaws brought their horses to a stop behind them next to the wagon. 'Maybe ya ain't bin telling us the truth about that treasure. Maybe there never was a damn treasure waiting for us to just pluck up and take back to civilization. Well?'

Barton could still see the insanity in the face of the gunman and considered his answer carefully.

'There's a treasure, OK,' he bluffed with all the skill of a Mississippi riverboat gambler. 'Waiting for us at Whispering Skull.'

Sharky looked all around them. His eyes seemed either unable or unwilling to blink any longer. He then saw the faces of the other outlaws and chuckled. 'Them boys look plumb feared, Jardine.'

'They got good reason,' Barton replied. He pointed at the gun in Sharky's hand. Smoke was still issuing from its hot barrel.

Behind them Pecos Bill had stood on the driver's board and was looking over the dense bank of white fog that faced them. The outlaw raised his voice to full pitch.

'Damn it all, Jardine. Ya done led us into a box canyon,' he shouted. 'There ain't no way out of here but going backwards and retracing our tracks. Damn it all. My wheel rims are barely hanging on now.'

'Box canyon?' Sharky growled.

'I figured we might have taken the wrong canyon,' Barton said calmly.

'Ya did?' Sharky fumed. 'Thanks for telling me. Which way do ya figure we oughta go to find the right route, boy?'

Barton touched his ear. 'Listen up.'

'What?'

'The sound seems to be louder over there, Sharky.' Barton tapped his spurs and steered his mount into the swirling mist.

Each of the outlaws watched Barton.

'Which way should we go?' Sharky repeated.

Barton gigged the tired horse to walk towards the canyon wall where the strange noise did seem to be slightly louder. Then to his complete surprise he saw something none of the others had as yet seen. It was a natural fissure more than twenty feet high and about eight feet wide at its base. It was concealed by the dense moving fog to everyone but Barton himself. The outlaw held his mount in check and studied the crack in the rocks carefully. It was dark but there was a glimmer of light at the far end of the natural tunnel.

'Which way should we go, Jardine?' Sharky yelled at the man he could no longer see.

'Thisaway,' Barton replied, then he spurred his horse.

'Ya led us into a damn box canyon, Jardine,' Sharky snarled like a venomous rattler ready to strike. He raised his .45 and waved it around.

Elam rode forward. 'He's gone.'

'What ya mean, he's gone, Elroy?' Sharky boomed.

'He's up and high-tailed it,' Tyler glossed.

Rance Lee spurred his horse to

where Barton had been only a few moments before. He spotted the well-hidden cleft in the rockface.

'The boys is right, Sharky. Jardine done found a tunnel and he's gone.'

Pecos Bill ran along the flatbed of his wagon and leapt down to the ground. He ripped his reins free of the tailgate and threw himself up on to the saddle. He rode up to the still open-mouthed Sharky.

The seasoned outlaw hit Sharky across the arm. 'Well? Is ya gonna sit here catching flies or is ya gonna go after Jardine, boy?'

Sharky was totally befuddled. 'What?'

'Look, Sharky. He done rode into this cave or whatever it is,' Lee said. He pointed his trigger finger at the place from where the strange sound still taunted them. 'He's gone, OK.'

The expression on the face of the deadly outlaw changed.

Changed from one of total anger to one of total insanity.

'What ya say, Rance?' Sharky hissed.

He spurred back to the others with Pecos Bill at his side. 'Did ya say he's gone?'

Lee gestured. Sharky leaned forward and saw the dark cleft in the rockface.

'Damn his stinking hide,' the outlaw raged. 'I knew he was bluffing. I just knew he was waiting for a chance to vamoose.'

'Gotta admit that Jardine's smart,' said Pecos Bill with a grin.

Sharky snarled and then spurred savagely. 'C'mon.'

The outlaw had no idea where the tunnel he was galloping through led, but that made little difference to him. All he wanted to do was escape before the rest of the gang realized that he had been leading them on a wild-goose chase. Now there was a chance to find freedom. It was slim, but it was the only one to have presented itself in all the long hours since they had left the lake of salt.

Barton spurred and thundered through the dark split in the mountain side. It was a long dark tunnel but there was a blinding light at its end. A light he knew was made by the sun. Drawn like a moth to a naked flame Barton feverishly whipped the tails of his reins across the back of his charging mount whilst driving his spurs deep into the animal's flesh. He had to keep his horse moving towards the light.

He had to reach the light, he told himself over and over again. He had to reach the light before the others managed to get him in their gun sights.

The sound of their pursuing hoofs suddenly filled his ears as they echoed all around him. He cursed himself and his followers with equal ferocity. He knew he had needed more time. More time to travel the length of the dark tunnel and reach the light before they caught up with him. Barton spurred and leaned over the neck of his charging horse.

'Keep going, boy,' he urged. 'Reach the light. Just reach the damn light before they open up with their hoglegs.'

The long fissure turned and twisted as the unholy sound travelled on the breeze and mocked his ears. With almost closed eyes Barton kept pressing onwards towards the unknown.

What lay ahead in the sunlight?

What would the other outlaws do to him when they caught up with him? Barton's mind screamed the question.

Would there be a way of escaping their revenge?

Again he spurred. Again the horse increased its pace. Again the sound of his pursuers grew louder. They were closing in on him, he thought.

'Jardine,' Sharky yelled out furiously. 'I'm gonna kill ya.'

Barton knew the outlaw meant it.

The horse kept heading towards the light. Now the sound of the wind was so loud that it drowned out the thundering of the hoofs that were gaining on him. Barton put his weight on to his left stirrup, turned and looked back. He could not see them but knew they were now too close. Then he saw the gun in Sharky's hand as the light found the devilish outlaw.

He swung on to his saddle and jabbed both his boots back so that his spurs hit the flanks of the horse as hard as they could.

His horse increased its speed yet again.

'That's the way,' Barton screamed. He stood in his stirrups and tried to lean as far as he could over the head and neck of his mount without toppling over his saddle horn and falling to his death. 'Keep going. Ya almost there.'

The horseman was coming nearer and nearer to the light. It was so close he could almost touch it. It was blinding, but he knew he had to reach it for it was his only hope of salvation.

Gripped by fear Barton whipped his reins across the rump of his galloping mount. The end of the tunnel was within spitting distance, he thought. Another thirty feet and he would be there.

Then he heard it.

The deafening sound of a gun being fired.

The tunnel lit up for a brief moment as the flash of a bullet sped just past his shoulder. Another shot followed. It had come even closer to its target. Then, just as the horse reached the bright sunlight, another shot was fired. This time it found a target. The horse gave out a pitiful whinny and crashed into the ground. Barton found himself hurtling over the creature's neck and rolling across the sand. He was dazed but still able to get to his feet.

Barton steadied himself and felt the heat of the sun on his shoulders. His eyes were almost closed as they tried to cope with the bright light but even so he could see that his mount was badly wounded. The creature lay on the sand as its life blood spread out around it.

The rays of the high sun beat down and Barton swung on his heels, trying to see if there was somewhere to hide. There was nothing but sand all around him. He was standing in a circle of sand as large as a bullfighting ring. The area was completely surrounded by high rocks. The only way in or out of this place was the natural crack in the rocks through which he had just ridden. Again he was trapped.

The sound of the riders grew louder. Barton turned to face the fissure. There was nothing else he could do. He had to wait for their arrival.

The noise of the pounding hoofs grew more intense and then they emerged in single file out of the darkness into the bright sunshine. They were upon him. The five remaining members of the gang which had once borne his name drew leather less than twenty feet from the spot where he stood. Just like Barton they all shielded their eyes waiting for them to adjust.

Instinctively Barton's hands went down to his hips and searched for the guns which Sharky and the others had denied him from having.

'Damn it all.' Barton turned and was

about to run when suddenly he saw the high wall of rocks that faced them. The outlaw rubbed his eyes.

Within a heartbeat Sharky and the others had dismounted and were standing right behind him.

'I'll teach ya to try and high-tail it, Jardine,' Sharky snarled. He drew his fresh gun from its holster and cocked its hammer. 'I knew ya was full of bull. Now I'm gonna blow ya head clean off ya shoulders.'

Barton did not flinch. His arm rose and he pointed up to the towering spires before them.

'Before ya kills me take a look up yonder, Sharky,' Barton drawled in almost as much disbelief as he knew would soon fill the others. 'What does that look like to you?'

Sharky blinked hard until his eyes obeyed him. He lowered his gun and slid it back into its holster.

'I . . . I don't believe it.'

'What don't ya believe?' Tyler asked, rubbing his gloves over his eyes.

Sharky shook his head in disbelief. 'Look yonder, boys.'

They looked and then they saw.

An array of crumbling rocks towered high above the small gulch. Countless years had sculpted the shape of a skull at its very pinnacle. Holes resembling eyes allowed the wind to pass through them creating an unholy noise which chilled even the toughest of souls. As the outlaws stared up in wonder the bright sun moved behind the skull, sending two shafts of blinding light down and across the chasm.

'The Whispering Skull,' Sharky gasped.

'I told ya I'd lead ya here,' Barton said.

One by one the outlaws turned and looked to where the bright beams rested. Behind them the entire side of the canyon wall was not of the pinkish sandstone they had grown used to, but was of another, more intoxicating hue. It had a metallic tint that reflected the beams of sunlight until they danced and dazzled.

From the canyon floor right up to the tips of the jagged peaks the whole wall was shining like a well-polished mirror of gold.

Sharky staggered in disbelief towards it.

'Gold!' he gasped.

Barton nodded. 'Yep. The treasure of the Whispering Skull.'

Finale

It had been less than an hour since Sharky Cole had unleashed his fury and vainly attempted to destroy the rising fog bank with his usually lethal bullets. But that had been time enough for Captain Hyde to lead his men along the canyon and come across the abandoned wagon left by the outlaws after they had ventured into the black fissure. During that short time the merciless sun had sucked out every last droplet of moisture from the boulders and rock-faces. Now the early-morning mist had disappeared, like the ghosts of all those who had perished in this perilous place.

Hyde raised a white gauntlet and stopped his small band of horsemen as they drew close to where the wagon and its team of exhausted mules rested. The officer glanced back at the man they had saved from the deadly mountain ledge who was riding one of their pack animals. The young cowboy eased himself off the back of the mule and dropped to the ground. He had no idea what was happening but he was grateful that the soldiers had taken the time to rescue him from almost certain death.

'Dismount,' Hyde ordered, He stepped gracefully down from his high saddle and approached Stewart. He looked the ragged figure up and down. 'You will remain here, Mr Stewart.'

The cowboy shrugged. 'Where you headed, Captain?'

Hyde turned and stared at the abandoned wagon. 'I'm going to try and find the outlaws who left that prairie schooner there, young man.'

Riley moved between the two men. 'And I'm going with ya, Captain'

'I am going alone, Sergeant,' Hyde contradicted. 'This is a personal matter which does not require you or any of the men to risk their lives.'

The burly sergeant grinned. 'I'm still going with ya, Captain.'

Stewart could see that Hyde was not going to argue the case with his muscular sergeant. Both men nodded at one another and then Hyde looked at the six younger troopers.

'I want you men to get cover here and kill any of the outlaws who might happen to get past Sergeant Riley and myself.'

Stewart watched as the soldiers started to load their weaponry and the two older men slowly approached the wagon. The cowboy drew his own gun and stared at it for a few moments. He wondered if it was still capable of firing.

* * *

The cunning Jardine Barton had been spared death by some incredible twist of fate. Somehow everything he had invented years earlier to keep his gang in tow had suddenly become reality. Barton stared at the wall of golden rock in utter disbelief. His men had been investigating the beautiful, gleaming formation since they had followed him into the strange box canyon. The outlaw walked to the body of his horse, pulled its canteen free and unscrewed its stopper. He drank slowly as he began to realize that the others were not going to execute him after all. One strange heavenly intervention had saved his bacon. He moved along the line of horses and listened to the outlaws in amused silence. He reached Tey Tyler's white gelding and hung the canteen on its saddle horn. As he did so Pecos Bill's voice rose higher than all of the others.

'This ain't gold,' Pecos Bill announced.

Each of the men stopped talking and looked at their older cohort. Sharky Cole tilted his head and glowered at him.

'Are ya loco, Pecos?' Sharky growled.

Pecos Bill ambled towards the others. 'I ain't loco. I panned for gold a whole heap of years back, Sharky. I knows real gold and I knows fool's gold.'

Barton glanced at the saddle beside which he was standing, across at the others. Each of them had a well-oiled rifle stock poking out of a scabbard. With dread starting to roil inside his guts Barton listened and kept staring at Tyler's Winchester, which was only a few inches from his fingers.

Sharky gestured at the towering wall of glistening rock, then stared hard at Pecos Bill. 'Ya fooling with us, right, Pecos Bill? Ya just having yaself some fun. This is real gold OK. Just look at it.'

'It's fool's gold, Sharky,' Pecos Bill repeated. 'Ain't worth a plug nickel.'

'Fool's gold?'

'Yep.'

'Are ya sure?'

'Yep.' Pecos Bill sighed. 'Dead sure.'

Sharky began to shake like a volcano about to erupt. His stained teeth gritted together and he turned to where Barton was standing.

Before any of them could open their mouths Barton started to fire his newly acquired Winchester. With deadly accuracy Barton demonstrated that he had not lost any of his once-famed deadly expertise with a rifle.

Pecos Bill was the first to be knocked off his feet by the lethal volley of lead. As he fell dead Tyler was buckled by his own weapon's bullets. He twisted and then slid down the golden wall of worthless rock. Elam and Lee decided that the best form of defence was to attack but before they had taken three strides both gunmen had been slain. Sharky Cole had drawn both his guns and started to fire through the gunsmoke. Then he felt his body being punched as bullets tore into him.

Yet, even mortally wounded, Sharky was not going to quit. With both his six-shooters blazing the outlaw staggered away from his dead comrades and homed in on Barton.

'Ya gonna die this time, Jardine,' he proclaimed.

Bullets whizzed to either side of Barton. A horrific whinny rang out as

Tyler's horse was hit and fell behind Barton.

'Too close, Sharky.' Barton pushed the hand guard down. A spent casing flew out of the rifle and landed beside the dozen others he had discharged. He jerked the lever back up. He raised the Winchester and stared through its sights along its length.

Sharky was still approaching. Still firing.

'Don't ya know when ya dead, Sharky?' Barton screamed. His finger squeezed the rifle's trigger. The last of its bullets exploded from the barrel through a deafening cloud of smoke.

The bullet hit Sharky's temple just below the hat brim. The back of his skull erupted in a mess of gore. Sharky was sent flying backwards. A cloud of dust rose around the body as blood spread from the lifeless outlaw.

Barton threw the empty rifle away and walked to the nearest of the bodies. Elam had taken two perfectly placed shots to his chest. He lay open-eyed with his .45 in his gun hand as the last survivor of the Barton gang removed the gun and belt from the corpse.

The exhausted Barton strapped the belt around his hips, loaded the six-gun and made his way to the horses. He grabbed the reins of Elam's mount, stepped into its stirrup and hoisted himself up on to the saddle.

He swung the horse around and spurred for the dark cleft in the rockface. The horse and rider entered the natural fissure in the wall of solid rock and headed back to where Barton knew the wagon and its supplies awaited.

As he thundered through the echoing tunnel Barton started to laugh out loud.

*   *   *

Hyde and Riley had only just reached the wagon when suddenly they heard the pounding of hoofs coming from the well-hidden cavity in the rocks. Both men took cover behind the wagon's lowered tailgate. Riley readied his rifle whilst Hyde lifted the flap covering his revolver and withdrew it silently.

'Get down, Captain.' The words had barely left Riley's lips when the horseman appeared.

Barton saw the sergeant crouching, cocked his gun hammer and fired. Riley went tumbling backwards. His superior officer narrowed his eyes and glared at the rider. He had seen the likeness of the deadly outlaw many times over the years. It was an image which was branded into his mind.

'Barton!' Hyde exclaimed.

The outlaw dragged back on his reins as he spotted the cavalry officer moving away from the wagon. He had cocked his gun hammer again just as Stewart came galloping up from the line of troopers astride one of their mounts. At first Barton thought that it was a stray horse but then the truth dawned upon him.

With an expertise that only cowboys

ever truly master Stewart rode straight at the outlaw whilst virtually hidden from view. He was balancing on his left stirrup and clinging to the side of the horse. As the animal rode between Hyde and Barton, the cowboy heaved himself up the side of the horse, stepped on the saddle and leapt the distance between the outlaw and himself.

The cowboy caught Barton around the shoulders.

Both men rolled over the saddle cantle and crashed to the ground. Barton smashed his gun barrel across Stewart's face and sent the cowboy reeling.

Hyde's voice rang out. 'Barton.'

The outlaw raised himself up on one knee and cocked his gun hammer again. Through the dust kicked up by the bucking horse he could see the officer walking towards him with his own gun drawn.

Barton levelled the .45 and aimed.

A chilling shot rang out. Its sound

echoed all around the canyon. Hyde stopped moving. He simply watched as the outlaw fell dead on the ground.

Riley crawled back to the side of his superior. 'Ya got the evil bastard, sir.'

'Not me, Sergeant,' Hyde said.

As the dust cleared both men were looking at the cowboy. In his hand the ancient smoking gun told the truth.

'That young cowpoke killed him?' Riley said. He rose up on his feet, nursing his wounded shoulder.

'Indeed.' Hyde pushed his gun back into its holster and then saluted Stewart. 'He also saved my life.'

Jeff Stewart got back to his feet. His hand was shaking as he holstered the gun. He returned the salute and then smiled.

THE END